The Lake War

Kinkaid with the Inland Fleet

Michael Winston

Copyright 2013

An adventure in the continuing saga of Jonathan Kinkaid of the American Navy

Preface

It is the summer of 1776. The Declaration of Independence has just been signed, and the first and largest battle of the Revolution has been fought on Long Island, forcing General Washington's army to retreat. Meanwhile a large British army under General Guy Carleton has landed in Montreal and means to push south through the chain of lakes and waterways to join with Major General William Howe in New York City. The only thing standing in their way is General Benedict Arnold's ragtag bunch of Continentals, militia and seamen at the bottom of Lake Champlain.

While General Arnold may be best known as a traitor to the American cause, he was also one of our best and most active Generals before he met that Loyalist gold-digger Peggy Shippen and made the worst mistake of his life.

Not only did he bravely lead the Continental Army to victory at the Battle of Saratoga and command a daring but ill-fated attack on Quebec City, but as a colonel early in the war he joined forces with Ethan Allen to recapture Fort Ticonderoga, sending most of the fort's cannons to Boston where they were used to force the British to abandon the city.

Later, he became the military commander of Montreal but was forced to retreat when a large British force arrived. Even then he showed his fortitude and resolve by ingeniously building an inland fleet at the bottom of Lake Champlain in order to stop the British from sailing down the chain of lakes and dividing the colonies. This was the first arms race in American history. Here, too, was the first use of

American marines aboard ships.

Although Arnold's inland fleet was ultimately over-matched and defeated at the Battle of Valcour Island in the first naval engagement of the American Revolution, the effort paid off, for this little known but pivotal action served to delay the British advance long enough to give Continental forces the time to prepare and eventually defeat the British the following summer at the Battle of Saratoga, where Arnold bravely led the Continental troops to a great victory while General Gates sat in his tent but then claimed all the glory afterwards. Not only was the British General "Gentleman Johnny" Burgoyne forced to surrender his 7,000 man army, but the news of that victory was the chief reason that the French decided to join with us against the British, bringing an end to the war when their fleet showed up and blockaded Cornwallis at Yorktown.

Native Americans were a major factor during the Revolution, especially the Iroquois. Known as the Six Nations Confederacy, they tried to remain neutral in the white man's war, but the Battle of Oriskany split the loyalties of the tribes as members of the Seneca, Cayuga, Onondaga and Mohawk were enticed by the British to fight for them, while the Oneida and Tuscarora tribes sided with the rebels.

This is the story of Kinkaid's first assignment as a Continental Naval officer, whereby he is ordered to report to General Arnold in the north woods of New York State, and is as true a story as I've ever told.

Contents

I

Any and All Assistance

Jonathan Edward Kinkaid had been made a lieutenant only two months after the Continental Navy was officially founded by Congress last November. Since then he had been anxiously awaiting an assignment, and so it was exciting to finally receive the letter from the Marine Committee telling him to check into the Grand Hotel in Boston and await further instructions.

Well, he'd been waiting now for two days and was getting rather tired of lounging about the sitting room of the lobby, listening to businessmen discussing business and travelers talking inanely about the latest fashions or decide which restaurant they might go to that evening while he tried to read his newspaper. Not that the latest news wasn't of interest, for much had happened in the last year, although most of it had been bad news.

The battles of Lexington and Concord had taken place, as well as the Battle of Bunker Hill, attributed as a victory for the British even though they lost more than twice as many men as the rebels, but of course they had prevailed by their sheer weight of numbers, not to mention their vast fleet.

Since then a number of petitions to the King had been sent to England, only to bring more proclamations from the British Government to cease and desist all this rebellious behavior and stop talking about things like freedom and independence. And when this fell on deaf ears further rebellious behavior was met with martial demonstrations meant to terrorize the colonies into submission, such as the cruel and barbaric burning of Falmouth, all of which only served to escalate hostilities with retaliatory strikes by colonial forces under Montgomery and Arnold at Montreal and Quebec, both ending in disaster for the American cause.

At least Fort Ticonderoga had been retaken by Arnold and Allen, and the miraculous feat by Knox of shipping all those cannons from the fort to the heights above Boston had convinced General Howe to evacuate the city, and he had taken his army, navy, and almost a thousand loyalists with him to Nova Scotia.

But then he returned just as the Declaration of Independence was being signed, along with his brother Lord Richard Howe, in command of the fleet, and they attacked Washington's forces on Long Island, sending the Continental Army into retreat, and now the British occupied New York City.

Kinkaid was sitting in the same overstuffed chair in the corner by a window that he had been sitting in for the last two days, reading today's paper, specifically an article saying that a large British army had just landed at Montreal, when he heard her voice again, telling the desk clerk that she would wait for her mother in the sitting room.

It was a very lovely voice and there was also a very lovely face that went with it and he had found himself bringing both to mind quite often since he last saw her when she and her mother had first checked in. It was on the same day that he had checked in and he had helped them with their baggage.

He had little chance to speak with her then, except to learn that her name was Cornelia Webster and that she and her mother had come down from Wakefield to do some shopping, and since he hadn't seen either of them he assumed that they had checked out, and so it was nice to see her lovely face as she strolled into the sitting room.

"Good morning, Miss Webster."

"Oh, and a fine morning to you. You surprised me; I thought you had checked out."

"No, I'm afraid I'm still waiting." She was petite, with reddish hair under her bonnet, but it was her large pale eyes that held his attention.

"Well, I'm waiting as well, for my mother."

"Have a seat, then, and we can wait together," he said, gesturing to the empty chair next to him.

"Why thank you. I believe I shall."

The stilted moment of silence after she sat down had both searching for something else to say.

"I remember you said you were waiting for something, Mr. Kinkaid," she said, being the quicker of the two, "but I don't believe you explained exactly what that was."

"Perhaps I did not explain, but now that you ask I am hoping for an assignment. I am in the navy, you know."

"Of course. A captain, if I recall."

"Perhaps someday. No, I'm a lieutenant, actually."

"I see."

Once again the silence intruded, but now Kinkaid was able to come up with a new topic, sure to be of interest to the young woman.

"Have you and your mother been able to find some good bargains in the city?"

"Well, we haven't exactly come for the bargains, but for a few special things that we simply can't find in Wakefield."

"I see."

"What colors do you favor, Mr.—uh, Lieutenant Kinkaid, if you don't mind my asking?"

"Colors?"

"Yes."

"Well, I suppose I'm partial to blue," he answered, feeling foolish. Yet, he would have been the first to admit that even carrying on a foolish conversation with Cornelia Webster concerning colors was far preferable to not speaking with her at all, and so he stumbled on, "although red is also quite attractive, especially next to blue."

"Why, I believe you are describing your uniform," she pointed out.

Kinkaid looked down at his uniform coat with the red facing and had to admit, "Yes, I suppose I am."

"I was thinking of something subtle, and light…to be used as curtains."

"White is nice."

"Oh, but so common. I was thinking of something with just a hint of color, something that might add a warm glow to the harshest sunlight."

"Yellow, I suppose, would do that."

"It would, but then yellow is the color of dirty curtains, and we couldn't have that."

"No, of course not."

"Oh, but here I am speaking to you about curtains and you're worried about finding gainful employment. How foolish of me."

"Nonsense," said Kinkaid. "Curtains are important, too."

Fortunately, they both laughed at the same time.

"I believe you are quite shy, Lieutenant Kinkaid," she said

with a smile.

"Do you think so?" said Kinkaid, feeling like he would swoon.

"Yes, I do. But that is not a bad thing. In fact, it is far better than being brash and pushy."

"I would agree with that." At the moment he would have agreed to anything Miss Webster had to say; anything at all.

"What kind of an assignment are you hoping to find?"

"Well, a placement aboard a ship would be my first choice, of course, but since I have little in the way of seniority, I would not expect…"

Kinkaid noticed a young man wearing the uniform of a midshipman come into the hotel at that moment and it distracted him, but when he heard the young man say at the front desk, "I have a message for a Lieutenant Kinkaid," he jumped up from his chair like he was shot from a cannon.

"I am Lieutenant Kinkaid," he said. "If you would please excuse me, Miss Webster."

"But of course."

The handsome young midshipman saluted and said, "Pleased to make your acquaintance, Lieutenant. I am Midshipman William Weatherby, from the office of the Northern Naval Department. I was told to personally deliver this letter to you."

"Thank you, Mr. Weatherby," said Kinkaid, taking the envelope.

"My pleasure. And a good day to you, Sir," said the young man, and off he went.

Kinkaid was glad that the young man hadn't been instructed to await a reply, for he saw that his hands were trembling as he tore open the envelop and held the short note in his hand, Miss Webster for the moment all but forgotten, informing him that he was to report to the office of the

Northern Naval Command at precisely one o'clock on the following day, and an address was provided.

"Good news?" asked Miss Webster, coming over.

"I have a meeting tomorrow."

"Then it seems your waiting shall soon come to an end."

"Oh, if it isn't that nice young man who helped us with our baggage," said Miss Webster's mother, standing at the bottom of the stairs. She was a well-dressed woman with lovely features similar to her daughter, only a bit plumper. "I'd love to chat, but we really are late, so we'd better run along, Cornelia, my dear."

"Yes mother."

Their conversation had just begun to get interesting and now it would end all too soon, thought Kinkaid, but he bowed like a gentleman and said, "I hope you find the curtains you are looking for, Miss Webster, and I hope to see you both again very soon, Ma'am."

Once they had left Kinkaid read the note he had been given once again, and felt excited, in fact more than excited. Already it had been somewhat nerve-wracking, waiting expectantly over the last two days, and when he looked at the clock behind the front desk he quickly calculated that his appointment would take place in exactly twenty-six hours and twenty minutes.

He tried to finish reading the newspaper, but found that he had lost his concentration, his thoughts an equal proportion of Cornelia Webster and his anticipated meeting, and so he got up and went outside onto the street. There was a marketplace in a square not two blocks away and he headed in that direction, his mind occupied with all kinds of possibilities, both romantic and practical.

Of course he hoped that he would be assigned to one of the new frigates that he knew were being built, two in

Poughkeepsie and another two in Philadelphia. If so, being made gunnery officer would have been his first choice. But he would accept being put in charge of a sail division as well. Of course there was the possibility that he might even be assigned to the Northern Naval Command offices. And though it would not be very exciting, he at least hoped that they'd put him in a section dealing with operations or intelligence, and not in something humdrum like procurements.

But then he was probably the most junior lieutenant in the new navy and of course he would accept any position offered him, for it had been a torture waiting for the last six months to even be called to duty.

The marketplace was crowded with shoppers and passersby and while he thought that coming here would distract him from his apprehensions and expectations, it didn't work and he scarcely noticed the people strolling by or the fruits and vegetables piled on carts all around him. Instead he found himself heading toward the address provided in the note.

When he arrived at twenty-seven Congress Street some fifteen minutes later he found no sign on the door. Nor was there a guard standing outside, or even a flag hanging from an upstairs window of the two-story brick building. In fact, there was no indication at all that this was the Office of the Northern Naval Command and so he returned to the hotel where he partook of another desultory dinner, eating alone and having to listen to more businessmen discussing business.

Actually, the hardest thing was having to listen to young couples flirting and trying to impress one another, especially when they noticed him sitting by himself in a dark corner, wishing only to remain inconspicuous, and wishing even more that he was dining with Cornelia Webster, and so he tried hard not to look at them looking at him, the result being that he wolfed down his meal and left as quickly as possible.

But at least he knew where he was to go the next day and he knocked on the door at exactly seven minutes before the hour of one.

"Ah, it's Lieutenant Kinkaid," said the same young midshipman that had delivered Kinkaid's note. "Good afternoon, Sir."

The midshipman's name had since escaped him; William something, perhaps Weathers or Feathers, and since he was too embarrassed to ask he only returned the perfunctory, "Good afternoon."

"Please have a seat and I shall inform Captain Aldrich that you are here."

Kinkaid waited for another ten minutes, all the while fidgeting nervously with his buttons and adjusting his hair and making sure his uniform and shoes and nails were clean before he was ushered into the rather bare and cramped office of Captain Jacob Aldrich, who shook his hand cordially enough and got right to business.

"I'm sure you probably thought we'd forgotten about you," said the short, wiry captain, now deskbound and handing out assignments to other officers and captains, a job he probably resented or would grow to resent, thought Kinkaid, for he imagined that he would probably feel that way if he had been given such a position.

"I regret that we kept you waiting so long, Lieutenant. To tell you the truth, there are only so many positions available and too many officers to fill them, and well, we didn't really know where we'd put you until this news came to us just a few days ago about this force landing at Montreal to bolster Carleton's forces. And quite a considerable force, if you believe the reports of some of our people up there. As you might know General Sir Guy Carleton is both the Governor of Quebec as well as the Governor General of British North America, and so of course any considerable force that is sent to him must be taken seriously."

"Of course, Sir."

"Now then, we've received an urgent request from General Arnold, who has just been appointed by General Schuyler to oversee naval operations on Lake Champlain."

"I wasn't aware that we had naval operations on Lake Champlain, Sir," said Kinkaid, instantly regretting the question. First of all, it admitted he was not aware of something that he probably should have known about. Second, it sounded like he was dismissing naval operations on a lake as something trivial.

"Well, we've only just begun such operations…out of necessity, for Arnold seems to believe that the British will soon launch a considerable fleet from the northern end of the lake and employ the system of waterways to come down and join with Howe in the city, thereby effectively splitting the colonies."

"I see."

"And that must be prevented at any cost," said Aldrich, squinting his eyes rather harshly as he said it.

"Of course, Sir."

"Now, we're sending you up there with a number of seamen and ship's carpenters, all detailed to help build and man Arnold's ships and guns, as well an assortment of tools, equipment and supplies that Arnold should find useful. You will meet this group in the town of Tappan Zee on the Hudson and take charge of them. Of course there will be among this group a man to act as your orderly as well as one who will be familiar with the route that you should take to arrive at General Arnold's camp with all due haste. You will then report directly to General Arnold at Fort Ticonderoga in the capacity as an advisor in the building, manning and fighting of a fleet of ships meant to defend the lake against such forces as will oppose us. In other words you will provide General Arnold any and all assistance that it may be in your capacity as a naval officer to provide. Do you understand, Lieutenant?"

"Of course, Sir. I am to provide General Arnold any and all assistance that is within my capacity," repeated Kinkaid, while wondering what kind of assistance he might provide to a General of Arnold's stature, not to mention questioning what his capacity as a new lieutenant with no naval experience, might be.

"Now, here are your written orders," said Captain Aldrich, handing over a brown envelop wrapped with a red string. "I cannot impress upon you enough the need for utmost urgency in arriving at General Arnold's camp; therefore I have included the address of a stable where you will be provided a sturdy mount, along with enough supplies to sustain you on your journey. All you will have to do is sign for the animal. I assume you have enough uniforms and personal effects? If not, I advise you to equip yourself before you leave, for you will find few stores north of Tappan Zee until you get to Albany."

"I believe I already have most of what I need, Sir."

"Good. Oh, and I should tell that as far as providing anything that you or your men shall require as you set forth, there is an army encampment at West Point where you might procure any supplies or equipment that might help you ensure the success of your assignment. Now, do you have any questions?"

Kinkaid had plenty of questions, but could not think of one

that would not sound like he lacked confidence, and so he replied, "No, Sir."

"Well, then good luck to you, Lieutenant, and I am certain you will make a good account of yourself."

"Thank you, Sir. I shall do my best."

Kinkaid left the office in a daze, although mostly he was relieved that the interview was over.

When he arrived back at the hotel he was pleased to find that Cornelia Webster was sitting in the same chair where they had conversed the morning before.

"Waiting for your mother again?" he asked, giving her his best smile.

"Oh, Lieutenant Kinkaid," she said, standing and giving a slight curtsey. "How pleasant to see you again. How did your meeting go?"

Kinkaid wanted to tell her how much he had missed her since he last saw her. He also wanted to ask her to have dinner with him that evening, even if her mother had to come along. But instead he properly answered her question.

"I'm being sent to be an advisor to General Arnold."

"An advisor? My, that seems important."

"Well, I had wanted a ship," he said, but instantly regretted saying that for it made him sound like he was ungrateful.

"Well, an advisor is no small matter," she said, "and to a general, at that. They must think you quite an expert."

"Yes, I suppose they do," he answered, and suddenly he felt unsure of himself. He, an advisor? Why, the idea seemed preposterous.

"Cornelia?"

"Oh, there's mother."

"The coach is waiting, dear," said Mrs. Webster as she came into the sitting room.

"Good morning, Ma'am."

15

"Good morning, Lieutenant. Now say goodbye to the nice young man, Cornelia, for we really must be off."

Kinkaid's mind was racing as they stood there looking at one another, for there was so much that he wanted to say to her, and other things that he wanted to ask of her, but with her mother impatiently standing there, all he could manage was, "Did you find the curtains you were looking for?" He wanted to talk to her forever, about anything and everything under the sun. In fact, he never wanted their conversation to end.

"Oh, yes," said Cornelia happily. "And many other things, as well. All for the fine house that I shall soon be living in. I am to be married in a month, you know."

Kinkaid almost choked, but managed to say, "Well, then congratulations are in order."

"Why, thank you so much."

Their shopping expedition must have been quite successful, for Kinkaid could not help but notice that they were departing from Boston with considerably more baggage then when they had arrived. But he tried to keep a smile on his face as he graciously loaded it all onto the back of their coach and without even so much as a "thank you, sir," off they went, leaving him standing in front of the hotel like a lost sailor.

He went back inside and sat in the familiar chair in the corner of the sitting room by the window, and after spending a few moments considering what a fool he had been over Cornelia Webster, he was soon able to put the vision of her lovely eyes out of his mind and soberly consider what the Northern Naval Command had tasked him with.

Of course he had hoped to be assigned to a ship somewhere, anywhere, but instead they were sending him off into the north woods of New York State to General

Arnold of the Continental Army. And as an advisor, of all things, as if he could advise General Arnold about something he didn't already know about, a man who had started as a ship's captain and owner of his own vessel. Another consideration was that there seemed little chance for glory in such an assignment, as a naval officer stuck on a lake of all places, and there would certainly not be any chance to earn prize money. But then he'd also hoped that Cornelia Webster might have some place in his future. A flimsy thing, this thing called hope.

At least he hadn't been given an office job, and as a junior officer he had little choice in the matter, regardless, and so, deciding that he had little time to tend to a broken heart he stood up and went directly to the stable that Captain Aldrich had recommended, and there he found a helpful old man who provided him a sturdy mount that might take him to General Arnold's camp at Fort Ticonderoga. All he had to do was sign for it.

II

A Motley Crew

It had been quite some time since he had ridden a horse, and even then he had never ridden very far, and now every muscle in his body ached, so he was glad to see that he had finally reached the rendezvous.

And though it was reassuring to see the heavy-duty wagon in front of the tavern, pulled by a couple of stout oxen and piled high with all manner of ship-building tools and supplies, it was with some trepidation that Kinkaid got off the horse, stretched painfully, and then stepped up onto the front porch, for he had heard the raucous shouting and cheering from a block away, and nobody even noticed him when he stepped inside.

The White Stallion Tavern in the tiny village of Tappan Zee along the Hudson was filled with a bunch of loud and boisterous men of all ages, most of them soused to the gills and crowded at the bar where a stout man was balanced on the shoulders of two others, his head bumping the rafters, while the surrounding herd raised their mugs in a roaring toast.

"To our next hero; Big Ben Bowen!"

"Hip-hip-hurrah! Hip-hip-hurrah! Hip-hip-hurrah!"

Benjamin Bowen held a froth-filled mug that was so heavy that he had to hold it in both hands, and when he raised it to his lips he fell backwards off the shoulders of his supporters and landed with a resounding crash onto the bar, bringing a roar of laughter from the mob.

"Lordy, have I been shot?" asked the stunned hero.

"No need to worry, Ben, it's just a bar wound!" shouted one of the men who had dropped him, bringing another roar of laughter.

"Why, you've lost your refreshment," said another, picking up Ben's now empty mug off the plank floor, none the worse for wear.

"Refill, refill, refill!" chanted the crowd as the tavern keeper took the mug and commenced to refill it from the keg behind him.

Kinkaid made his way over behind the man called Ben, loudly cleared his throat and in his best topside bellow, roared, "Excuse me!"

All grew quiet and stared at him.

"If you are Sergeant Benjamin Bowen, then you are one of the men assigned to accompany me."

Big Ben straightened up at the sound of his name, and then his gray eyes grew wide and serious as he took in the man standing before him in the uniform of a Continental Navy officer.

"Why, you musht be Lieutenant Kinkaid," said Bowen, extending a hand.

"We salute officers in my branch of the service," said Kinkaid.

At that, Big Ben stood at attention and threw up his hand in a stiff salute, his elbow slamming into the jaw of the man standing next to him, knocking the man back and forcing his friends to catch him.

"Sergeant Benjamin A. Bowen, reporting as ordered, Shur."

Big Ben was a bear of a man, with a barrel chest and a big square head sitting on top of an oak trunk for a neck. His uniform was tight and patched here and there, and his armpits were stained with sweat, but the worst, other than being drunk as a skunk, was that he smelled like a slaughterhouse.

Kinkaid had been told that Sergeant Bowen would be in charge of a small coterie of militia that he had recruited himself, to accompany him up to Arnold's command on the lake. Having experience as a carpenter, blacksmith and butcher, Bowen was touted as a jack of all trades and deemed a useful sort to send up to help Arnold. More than this, Sergeant Bowen supposedly knew the way to Arnold's camp.

Kinkaid returned the salute, asking, "Where are the others?"

"All here, Shur," said the Sergeant, saluting again. "Fall in, men!"

Six men separated themselves from the carousing mob and quickly formed a line.

"Only six men?" said Kinkaid as he looked them over while they wobbled unsteadily.

"But good men, Shur; ash good as any dozen Continentals. All have some experience as carpenters," insisted Bowen, "and they're all pretty good marksmen, too, as I trained 'em myself," which brought as many chortles of skepticism as expressions of approval from the crowd.

They may have been good men, with the skills Sergeant Bowen mentioned, but they didn't look like much. Dirty and unshaven, and wearing only well-worn and frayed civilian clothes, they smelled as bad if not worse than their sergeant, and every one of them was at least half drunk.

Kinkaid thought at first that he would comment on how disorderly they appeared and tell them that they would have to shape up, but then thought better of it. First of all, if he was to be their leader he wanted to get off on the right foot with them. And then he had to consider that they had all been told to meet here at this tavern, and where there was a tavern there would surely be beer as well as men to buy it for them when they learned they'd be going off to war, if only to ease their own guilt over not going themselves. Yet it seemed to Kinkaid that at least they could have taken a bath and shown up wearing clean clothes for the beginning of their journey.

"I suppose six will have to do. Is every man properly equipped?"

"Each has a serviceable musket and cleaning kit, powder horn and cartridge case, bayonet with scabbard and belt, wadding and extra flints, one pound of powder and forty lead balls, a jackknife or hunting knife, a tomahawk, canteen, knapsack, and blanket."

"Is there anything they need? I was advised to stop at the army's garrison at West Point for anything we lacked."

"Well, the men could use some proper uniforms, Shur. And shoes."

"Very good, Sergeant."

Now a tall, thin man with a small pack on his back and a leather satchel looped over a shoulder elbowed his way through the crowd, saluted, and said, "I'm Corporal Joseph Sanderson, Sir, assigned to be your clerk and orderly."

Sanderson wore glasses and had a long, gray goatee that came to a point on his frail chest. He looked awfully fragile, and too old for army life. Like the others, his clothes were frayed and torn and hung on him like a scarecrow but at least they were clean, and his eyes were sharp and penetrating and he seemed to be sober.

"Pleased to make your acquaintance, Corporal Sanderson," said Kinkaid, returning the salute.

"And we're to go with you too, Sir," said a clear voice from a dark corner of the tavern.

The man who had spoken now stood up, along with another man, and the crowd opened as they both staggered forward from too much ale. Both wore the off-white, canvas bell-bottomed trousers of sailors, and both had a red scarf tied around their neck, but there the similarity ended.

"I'm Jack Parker, and this here is my mate, Patrick O'Toole. We're both able seamen, Sir."

Jack Parker was a fair-haired young man of about twenty, of average height, with pink and rosy cheeks, a winning smile and a pleasant voice. But what stood out was the way his white linen shirt was stretched taut over a muscular chest and massive biceps.

His mate, however, looked old, much older even than Sanderson. In fact, he looked ancient, probably going on sixty, with long white hair that was tied off at the back in an eel skin. But his stripped shirt and blue coat looked almost new, and he had a nice knife tucked into an embroidered scabbard on his belt. Overall, both men looked clean and squared away.

O'Toole calmly sucked on his fancy carved ivory pipe before explaining, "Actually, I'm a boatswain's mate, Sir. We come up from Boston after having to burn our ship to keep it from falling into the hands of the British."

"That's a hard thing to have to do," granted Kinkaid.

"Near broke my heart, Sir."

Kinkaid recalled what his orders had said; that "a number

of ship's carpenters and seamen will be detailed to help build and man Arnold's boats and guns." And here they were, numbering exactly two, thought Kinkaid sourly.

"No carpenter's mates?"

"Our carpenter's mate, Landry, and his work crew were hired at Jackson's boat yard on the Narragansett, where they're building a couple of privateers." Noting Kinkaid's disappointed look, the old boatswain's mate added, "Uh, we did bring a wagonload of supplies up with us, Sir. Ship-building tools, spars, seizing, spun yarn, cordage, water barrels, pulleys and fittings, stuff like that."

"I noticed. And I'm glad to have all of you," said Kinkaid diplomatically, "as I'm sure Arnold will be glad as well. Now then, no use in wasting the day. Are we all packed and ready to go?"

"Aye, Lieutenant," said O'Toole.

"Then let us form up outside and be on our way, men."

And with that they all went outside, followed by the men in the tavern.

"Private Metcalf, bring our supply wagon up," said Bowen.

Private Metcalf was about the sloppiest and stinkiest soldier in the bunch, with rotten teeth and torn and tattered clothing that hadn't been washed in months, it seemed, but he followed Sergeant Bowen's order without a word and went to the back of the building in his torn and floppy hat to where a wagon pulled by two big blue roans waited, and he promptly drove the wagon to the front of the tavern and pulled it up behind the wagon the sailors had brought.

Sergeant Bowen looked at the sailor's wagon, and noticing the four large barrels in the back, asked, "What's in those barrels?"

Able Seaman Jack Parker was about to answer when the

old man, O'Toole, grabbed him by the arm and said, "Why, that's water."

"Water?" said Sergeant Bowen in consternation. "Now, why in God's name are you carrying water? There's plenty of good clean water between here and Lake Champlain. Why, there are streams and rivers and lakes full of it. Barrels of nails would have been a better choice."

"Well, in case we only find bad water we'll have good sweet water with us," said O'Toole. "But we got nails, too. And spikes."

"Water. I never heard of such a thing."

"It's good sweet water," said O'Toole. Then he poked young Jack Parker in the ribs and asked, "Ain't that right, Jack?"

"The best and sweetest water you ever tasted," said Jack.

"Form up, men," ordered the sergeant, shaking his head in disgust, whereupon Bowen's six militia soldiers commenced to grab up their muskets, powder horns and cartridge cases out of the back of their wagon and then formed up alongside it with their muskets on their shoulders.

The wagon that the soldiers had brought was filled to overflowing with carpenter and blacksmith tools, various boxes, four long wooden crates of the kind muskets were transported in, a couple of rolled up canvas tents, an iron campfire grate, half a dozen cooking pots and pans, sacks of grain for the horses, as well as numerous packs and sacks containing everything from food and dry goods to personal belongings.

"We've enough provisions to last us a week or so, Sir," said Sergeant Bowen.

"That should be just about right, then," said Kinkaid.

"And I got four cases of muskets, too, if'n the sailors want a couple."

"We'll see to that later, Sergeant," said Kinkaid, wanting to get going, for he had been advised to arrive at General Arnold's camp with all due haste. "And you might have your men ride…it'll be a long trip."

"Very well, Sir," said Sergeant Bowen with a frown, as if lamenting the fact that his men would not be marching. "You heard the Lieutenant, men; jump up in back!"

Judging by their expressions the men were more than happy to toss their weapons and equipment back into the wagon and then climb up and find a perch on top of the pile of supplies.

Corporal Sanderson, however, remained standing beside the wagon, as if unable or perhaps reluctant to jump up into the back of the wagon with all those smelly men, and when Kinkaid looked his way the man said, "I'd as soon walk, Sir."

"Corporal Sanderson, why don't you ride on the seat next to Sgt. Bowen," suggested Kinkaid, thinking that the old man they assigned as his orderly wouldn't be able to walk very far or very fast and he didn't want him slowing them down.

"Thank you, Sir."

"And as far as your duties are concerned, you will kindly keep a log noting our progress and any salient events along our route."

"Very good, Sir."

Corporal Sanderson obligingly took a seat on the bench next to Sergeant Bowen while Kinkaid walked over to where his horse waited.

He didn't relish getting back into the saddle so soon, especially since he had already been riding for two hours that morning. But they had given him a good horse, at least, easily managed, and pretty, too; marble colored, with dark speckles. And now he hoisted himself back into the saddle and rode to the front of the two wagons.

Sergeant Bowen then stood up from his seat, and turning to the crowd of men on the porch of the White Stallion Tavern, he announced in a loud voice, "Well, we're off to the north woods, boys!"

"Give 'em hell, Ben!" shouted one of his friends.

"Bring us back a scalp or two!" shouted another.

And with that Kinkaid nudged his horse and started down the road, followed by the two wagons, two sailors, a clerk, a sergeant, and a small detachment of six militiamen, ten men in all. Not much of a command, but at least up front he wouldn't have to march in their stench. God, the soldiers stank.

They soon reached the edge of the village and then the road meandered through a mile of fields of chest-high corn, knee-high wheat, potatoes, carrots and beets, where stately maples lined the road.

It was late in the morning, sunny but still cool, and very quiet, the only sound being the jingle of the harnesses and the sound of the birds singing, and after a while Corporal Sanderson began to imitate their songs.

Then Boatswain O'Toole started identifying the various songs while smoking his fancy pipe. And since Kinkaid happened to be riding alongside their wagon, O'Toole explained, "I learned all my bird calls from the Indians, Sir."

"Is that so," said Kinkaid noncommittally before he nudged his horse and returned to the front of the column, uncomfortable with the easy familiarity of a naval officer bereft of a ship and thrown together with these strange men, the soldiers seeming most unmilitary.

So this was the crew they'd assigned to him, thought Kinkaid, with nobody saying much of anything because they knew they were still half drunk and didn't want to appear disrespectful in front of their superior.

And what a motley crew, he thought. But then actually they were really no crew at all, for a crew is what a group of men who serve aboard a ship are called, and of course there was never much chance of him getting assigned to a ship. Even had there been one available, they were usually officered and manned by men who knew somebody, or who had distinguished themselves already, and he possessed neither of these advantages.

But he tried to be positive about his situation, telling himself that he was lucky to have been given at least something to do whereby he might gain some distinction for future reference. It's just that he could not see how he might do that at the moment, nor could he fathom how he might do so in the future, by leading ten men up to some lake in the north woods to assist some army General in the building of some boats.

About the time that Kinkaid started to feel hot and sweaty from riding out in the sun like that, they came to the end of the fields and stately maples and entered a forest. It was late in the summer, the trees were filled out and heavy with leaves, and it was like the road went into a tunnel, a tunnel into a mountain of green, where it was cool, dark and quiet, and where nary a songbird was heard, but with chickadees, titmice and woodpeckers flitting from tree to tree.

They rode all that morning and after taking a ten minute break they rode most of the afternoon. At one point they came to a fork in the road and Sergeant Bowen said they should take the left fork, but then after about fifteen minutes he changed his mind and had them backtrack, mumbling something about being given faulty directions, before having them take the right fork, and it wasn't easy getting the wagons turned around, and now Sergeant Bowen's wagon was in the lead.

Later in the afternoon they finally came out of the woods where the Hudson River blocked their way. The road came to a T where another road ran parallel with the river, but this time Sergeant Bowen seemed to know where he was going and he confidently turned the wagon to the left. They hadn't gone more than a quarter of a mile before they came to a shack where two men ran a ferry.

Sergeant Bowen jumped down from the wagon and said to Kinkaid, "They'll want to charge us an arm and a leg to get across, Lieutenant, so let me handle this."

Well, it seemed like a miracle, but Sergeant Bowen had come with a special chit signed by an officer, saying that the ferrymen were "to be reimbursed for any reasonable charges by any command post of the Continental Army for conveying these men and their wagons across the river."

There was just one snag. The man in charge of the ferry looked like a stubborn man and sure enough, he said he didn't quite trust that the chit would be honored and so a big argument broke out between Sergeant Bowen and the stubborn ferryman that went on for some time.

Kinkaid just stood back and watched them yelling and hollering at each other. He had a letter signed by some colonel, saying that he was authorized to obtain any needed military supplies from the garrison at West Point, but nobody had given him a chit for a ferry ride and he didn't know anything about it.

But soon it began to worry him because he noticed that Sergeant Bowen's face was getting awfully red from all the arguing, and the veins on the Sergeant's face and neck started to swell up. They looked about ready to pop when the stubborn man's partner intervened and said, "Hell,

Charlie, we might as well take them across. We ain't got nothin' better to do at the moment, and besides, if we refuse to take 'em the army might get mad at us and not use our services any more."

It was a good thing, too, thought Kinkaid, because he could tell by Sergeant Bowen's red face and swollen veins that he wasn't going to take too much more argument before he might have resorted to his fists in order to settle the matter, something that must have occurred to the stubborn man's partner to make him speak up like that.

Well, the idea may have occurred to the stubborn man too, for he suddenly changed his mind, shook his head, pulled the chit paper that had some officer's signature at the bottom out of Sergeant Bowen's massive hand and said, "Oh hell, get aboard then."

So the first wagon was loaded onto the large flat raft, and then the men climbed aboard, and they were pulled across the wide river, and about two hours later both wagons had been ferried to the other shore. It was late in the afternoon by then and as they started up the road Sergeant Bowen starting laughing. At first it started out as a small chuckle or two, but then it grew into an insane cackling like he'd lost his mind.

Kinkaid decided to ride back and ask, "Now, what can be the source of all this mirth, Sergeant?"

Tears rolled down the Sergeant's face as he answered, "That dumb jackass of a ferryman took my chit and let us pass for nothing! Why, I wrote that chit out myself and signed it as if I was an officer. Hahahahaha! Stupid ninnies! When they go to cash it in, they'll get nothing but 'thank you, but we know nothing about this chit'. Hahahahaha! What do you think of that, Sir?"

It may have been funny to Sergeant Bowen to pull such a

29

cheat, but it wasn't funny to Kinkaid and it wouldn't be funny to those hardworking ferrymen to learn they'd been cheated by a Sergeant in the Continental Army, those men who had been worried that the Army might get mad at them for not taking the chit in the first place. It was something to know about Sergeant Bowen, and he would think twice before letting him "'handle" something again in the future.

It was almost dark now and Kinkaid decided they might as well camp as long as the road followed close to the river, thinking that some of the men might want to wash their clothes, or even take a bath.

One of Sergeant Bowen's men, a rather sad-looking black man named Private Watkins, who never seemed to smile, cooked up a pretty good beef stew that evening, and after dinner he sent that sorry excuse for a soldier, Metcalf, down to the river to wash their big cookpot.

Well, Private Metcalf hadn't been gone long before he came running back to camp shouting, "Injins! Injins down by the river!"

Kinkaid ordered three men to remain behind to watch over their campsite while he went with Sergeant Bowen and all the others to investigate, and what they found was one lone Indian, soaking his moccasins in the river.

He was shirtless and wore a fringed breechclout and red leggings. Tucked into a belt around his waist was a long hatchet, bedecked with feathers. Around his neck was looped a string of colorful beads as well as a knife and scabbard. Wide bands of silver encircled his arms and a silver ring with a tiny bell pierced his nose. His hair was mostly shaven, with two eagle feathers sticking up on top and another hanging behind his head. On the bank behind him was a small parfleche with a red blanket draped over it.

What impressed Kinkaid most was that the man's stern

expression never changed as they came up behind him; in fact he completely ignored all those white men standing on the bank staring at him like a circus attraction as he pulled his moccasins out of the water and slid them on his feet all soaking wet. Then he sat down and gazed out over the river like he was fascinated by all the water going by.

That's when the old boatswain, the man named O'Toole came over and said to Kinkaid, "He's an Oneida Iroquois, Lieutenant, of the wolf clan. I can tell by the way he wears his feathers and the tattoo on his chest. Want me to have a word with him, Sir?"

"Well, if you can speak his language, ask him what he's doing here and where he's going."

O'Toole went down to the river bank and started talking to the Indian just like he was one himself, and using a lot of hand gestures too, and pretty soon he came back up the bank and said, "His name ain't easy to translate, Sir, but it's something like Man Who Left the Light and Went Under a Cloud. He says he works for the Continental Army and that he's heading up to General Arnold's camp on important business."

"Ask him what business he has with General Arnold."

"I already did, Sir. He says he won't tell me or anybody else, even on pain of death. Says he give his word that he wouldn't tell a soul, but that his words are for the General alone."

Sergeant Bowen heard all this and said, "To see General Arnold? Now, that sounds suspicious to me. Hell, I doubt that Arnold would have much use for a dumb Indian."

"Dumb Indian?" asked O'Toole. "What makes you say that?" having heard such foolishness from white men before, men who knew nothing about Indians except that they were afraid of them and made no distinctions from one Indian to the next.

"Well, just look at him, sittin' there in his wet moccasins, starin' off down the river like there weren't a thought in his head, like he don't even know we're here."

"He knows we're here all right. And that's a new pair of moccasins he just put on," explained O'Toole. "They soak a new pair before putting 'em on so's when they dry out they'll fit like a glove. Why, they're more comfortable than any pair of boots the army ever made, and I aim to trade me for a pair as soon as I find an Indian with a pair to spare."

"Well, I doubt he's going up to see Arnold," was the only thing Bowen could come up with, irked as he was by O'Toole's explanation.

"Then why would he say that?" asked O'Toole.

When nobody could answer that question, Kinkaid said, "Tell him that we are going up to see General Arnold, too, and ask him if he wants to come along with us."

"I wouldn't do that, Lieutenant," said Sergeant Bowen. "No, Siree, I wouldn't be tellin' him where we was going, and I surely wouldn't be askin' no redskin to join up with our party, Lieutenant."

"And what is your reasoning, Sergeant," asked Kinkaid, "especially since he's going to Arnold's camp?"

"Why, Sir, he'll likely scalp us in our sleep."

"Well, that is why we set a night watch," said Kinkaid with some irritation, "to prevent things like that."

"Hell, Lieutenant, what if he has his friends with him? Why, he could set them to ambush us along the trail somewhere."

"That is something to consider, Sergeant," admitted Kinkaid, "And what do you propose we do to prevent that?"

When Sergeant Bowen couldn't think of anything to say to that, Kinkaid asked, "O'Toole, what do you know about these Oneidas?"

"Well, out of all the tribes of the Six Nations the Oneidas and Tuscaroras are the only ones to side with us."

"And why is that?"

"Oh, I suppose that missionary, Samuel Kirkland had something to do with it; he lived amongst 'em for years. And of course the Oneidas have lived near rebel communities, although the Mohawks have lived among whites longer than any of them, but they feel a particular allegiance to William Johnson, and now Joseph Brant keeps 'em stirred up against us."

"Are they as dangerous as they look?"

"They do give a man a fright, don't they, Sir? It's all a part of their charm. They don't fight like us, standing in lines and facing one another like gentlemen. No, they'll likely kill you from ambush. Why, there's none better in a forest fight, and they make fine scouts and messengers. I'd say this one's probably got a message for General Arnold."

"You don't think he'd try to scalp us in our sleep?" asked Kinkaid, giving Sergeant Bowen a look.

"Oh, he might do that, Sir," said O'Toole with a sly grin, just for Sergeant Bowen's benefit, "but if anybody knows this country and the shortest route to General Arnold's camp, it'd be him."

"Tell him where we are going and ask him if he would be so kind as to join our party, to help show us the way."

"Can I promise him all the tobacco he can smoke, Sir?" asked O'Toole. "They're partial to tobacco and such an offer will be hard to refuse."

"Do we have a good supply of tobacco, Sergeant?"

"Oh, we have plenty of tobacco, Sir. But, Sir, now I don't want to seem obstinate, but all we have to do is follow the river all the way up to Glens Falls."

"But I understand that the road does not always follow the river due to numerous cliffs and marshes."

"Now, Lieutenant, I know the way as well as any damned Injin, and I…"

"That will be enough, Sergeant," said Kinkaid as O'Toole went back down the riverbank and started talking to the Indian again.

Hell, here they were, not more than eight miles from the White Stallion Tavern and already Sergeant Bowen had taken them up the wrong fork in the road, and how many more forks in the road would they come to over the next two hundred miles to Fort Ticonderoga? That one mistake early on as well as learning that Bowen had cheated those ferrymen had lessened Kinkaid's confidence in the man, in his honesty as well as his navigational abilities, and if that Indian knew the way, he'd be a welcome addition to their party, is the way Kinkaid thought about it, not wanting to take the chance of getting lost and being late getting to General Arnold's camp, this being his first assignment and all.

As it turned out, the Indian didn't say if he would go with them or not in spite of the promise of all the tobacco he could smoke. Not only that, but he must have become disgusted with all those white men staring at him like he was an exhibit at the zoo while he tried to enjoy the sight of the river flowing by as his moccasins dried, because he suddenly stood up and went off into the woods to get a little privacy and maybe make his own camp where he could cook up whatever it was that Indian's cooked up out on the trail.

With the disappearance of the Indian and their main distraction, Kinkaid decided it was a good moment to give a hint to the men.

"I have no objection to you men taking a swim this

evening, or you could take one early tomorrow morning, but I wish us to be on the road by sunup."

Most of them looked at Kinkaid like they had been insulted and so, in order to set an example, he peeled off his uniform and took a quick bath, whereupon three men followed suit and jumped in and splashed one another for a while until the last of the daylight had faded.

The next morning Corporal Sanderson, Able Seaman Jack Parker and Boatswain O'Toole went down to the river to wash up after breakfast and the sight of them acting like civilized men worked on the others until every man did the same, except that Private Metcalf only washed his mess kit and not himself, which prompted Privates Watkins and McDuff to grab him and toss him into the river, and it was a hilarious sight to see the shocked Metcalf retreating back up the bank like he'd been thrown into a fire and not into a cool, refreshing river. Even the sad-looking Private Watkins broke into a grin when he saw that.

It was about a half hour after the sun rose by the time they hit the trail again. They hadn't gone more than a mile before they came out of the woods to an area of grassy meadows where a farm had once been hacked out of the wilderness, and that is when O'Toole handed the reins of their wagon to young Parker and jumped down and ran ahead to collect some leaves from a cluster of flowering Joe Pye weed alongside the road.

That is when they all noticed that same Indian again, standing in the road about two hundred yards ahead of them. This time there was a dog with him, a rather large brown dog with big floppy ears. But they didn't linger. Instead the Indian and his dog started jogging up the road and soon disappeared around the next bend.

"I'd say he's trying to decide if we're respectable enough

company for him, Lieutenant," offered Boatswain O'Toole, returning to the wagon with his collected leaves.

"Well, how long will it take him to decide?"

"I couldn't tell you that, Sir, but at least he stopped to check on us, and that's a good sign because he could have been twenty miles ahead of us by now, seein' as how they usually run wherever they're goin', especially if they have an important message to deliver. Now, if he picks up the pace and we don't see him for a day or two, then you'd have to conclude that he just don't care for our kind of company, Sir."

"How do you happen to know so much about the Indians, O'Toole?"

"Oh, I've lived with different varieties of them over the years, Sir. Learned the medicinal uses of plants from them, too, and you never know when that kind of knowledge comes in handy," he said, holding up his handful of leaves and then stuffing them into his pouch.

Kinkaid had a chance to listen to some of the stories that O'Toole told him about his life with the Indians as he rode alongside the sailor's wagon. He especially had to laugh when O'Toole told him about one particular Chief that wanted him to marry his daughter, except that she was so mean and ugly that O'Toole had to move on or be forced into marrying her.

After repacking his pipe, O'Toole concluded, "Yup, I coulda had an easy life, Sir, marryin' a chief's daughter. Hell, I could be loungin' around a campfire right now, bein' waited on hand and foot, with not a care in the world…except I'd have to wake up to that mean and ugly face every mornin'."

"How mean and ugly was she?"

"Well…think of a wildcat mixed with a bullfrog, Sir."

They kept seeing the Indian and his dog every now and again as the day wore on, just far enough ahead of them so that it seemed like he was keeping them in sight while he made up his mind to join them or not. But by the time it grew dark enough to make camp, it seemed that he was long gone.

Which made Sergeant Bowen so nervous that he set double the guard that night, to Boatswain O'Toole's amusement?

III

West Point

The night passed quietly enough and after a quick breakfast they were on the road by sunrise. It was a pleasant day and they made good time, and as it began to grow dark they had reached the palisades at West Point, where four soldiers at a lean-to along the road stopped them.

"Halt, who goes there?"

"Friends!" returned Kinkaid.

"Come forward, then, and be seen!"

Kinkaid rode closer until he could recognize their faces.

"I'm Captain Gilroy," said a young man in a dark blue coat with a red facing, white waistcoat and overalls. He wore a cockaded hat and had a long scar running across his cheek that was still pink, showing that it had only recently healed.

"Lieutenant Kinkaid, of the Continental Navy."

"You don't say. We don't see many of you navy types up this way. Did you get lost, Sir?"

"I'm taking this group and some equipment up to General Arnold's camp."

"I see."

"I was also advised that I might obtain whatever supplies we might need from this post. I have a letter to that effect."

The Captain chuckled and said, "Well, I'll tell you, Lieutenant. We got all excited when we saw your wagons. Hell, we thought you were bringing *us* some supplies. Some reinforcements would have been welcome, too. But I suppose General Arnold has his needs."

"How many are you?"

"We're part of a company of forty-seven that were just sent here a week ago to fortify this position."

"All we would require are a dozen uniforms and some shoes, if that would not be too much to ask."

"A dozen uniforms and some shoes? Sir, you might as well be asking for the moon. I don't know who gave you that letter or thought we were running some kind of military warehouse up here, but I can tell you we have only what we brought with us. Truth be told; we're about out of everything."

"We can leave you some tobacco, if that'll help."

"Why, thank you, Lieutenant, some tobacco will help just fine. And we're more than happy to share our supper and campsite with you for the night."

"I was hoping you'd say that," said Kinkaid, climbing wearily down from his horse as the wagons clattered up.

West Point was an important strategic site where the river narrowed through the palisades on either side. Right on the edge of the cliff were a series of stone abutments that were still under construction where cannons had been emplaced, commanding access up or down the river.

The main army camp sat on the edge of the cliff, where the river could be seen down below, shimmering under the moonlight, and Kinkaid and his party were soon sheltered under a stand of tall pines.

The dinner that Captain Gilroy's soldiers provided consisted of beans with bacon and some quickbread that had been twisted around sticks and baked over an open fire, and now Kinkaid was seated on a stump at a fireplace with the captain.

"It's a good spot to camp," said Gilroy. "Up on these heights we get a nice breeze off the river that keeps our work cool and keeps the mosquitos away. Although I should apologize for the meal, Lieutenant. It's nothing fancy, but it'll stick to your ribs."

"Couldn't ask for better, Captain, and we thank you for your hospitality."

"And thank you for the tobacco, Lieutenant. We were about to resort to sticks and bark in our pipes."

"Say, did you or any of your soldiers happen to see an Indian come by today? He had a dog with him."

"No," answered Gilroy, "we didn't see any Indian with or without a dog, and I hope not to see any while we're here. Why do you ask?"

"We had an encounter with one yesterday. Claimed he worked for General Arnold and was heading up to his camp."

"Well, I wouldn't know anything about that, although I heard they had joined with the British."

"We heard they were at the Battle of Long Island last month."

"We were there, Sir, under Sullivan," said Gilroy. "I didn't see any Indians, though I heard later that Brant was there. But we seen enough Hessians that I don't ever want to see another one again. Hell, I watched 'em bayonet a dozen of our men who had surrendered."

"Must have been a terrible fight."

"It was a helluva mess, is what it was. General Sullivan was outflanked. Why, we couldn't tell where they were coming from and Sullivan was sending troops first one way and then the other. At one point we had British Regulars on one side and Hessians on the other. You couldn't blame the men for running, what with all the artillery they had, and those of us who stayed ended up fighting with our empty rifles, using them like clubs after we were overrun. That's how I got this," said Gilroy, pointing to the nasty scar on his cheek. "Well, General Sullivan got himself captured; hiding out in some corn patch is what I heard. Hell, I was lucky enough to get my company out of there, though we lost over sixty dead, wounded or taken prisoner. We retreated back to Brooklyn Heights but then got surrounded again. At least we had some artillery set up at that point and we pounded the hell out of them as they dug their trenches closer to us all that night. It rained like hell that night, too, Lordy, did it rain."

Captain Gilroy shook his head at the sad memory, and then said, "They just couldn't be stopped. Too many of them and they knew their business, I'll say that. We knew we were in for it when morning came, but thank God Washington didn't let it come to that, or we'd all be dead or rotting in some stinking British prison. No, we left our fires burning and he got all of us across the river during the night, 9,000 of us in all. Actually my company and I were still waiting for a boat to take us across by morning, but lucky enough a thick fog rolled in and the British never caught on and we got away, too."

"That is quite a story," said Kinkaid.

"My first taste of battle, and I hope you'll forgive me, Sir, but I have to admit that I wasn't impressed by our leadership. No, if we're gonna win this thing, we're gonna have to find some better leadership than Generals who can't tell where the enemy is coming from and then allow themselves to get captured...uh, in my humble opinion.

Even Washington was fooled as to where the main British thrust was coming from. And look at us now; forty-seven men sent up here to fortify and defend this place."

"I guess we're spread pretty thin all over," was Kinkaid's feeble response, knowing that the navy was in even worse condition, having few ships and practically no funding.

"I suppose there's no use in complaining about it, but we're gonna have to do better. We just have to."

It was a grim assessment of somebody who'd fought with Washington, and Kinkaid couldn't begrudge the man his opinion.

After more than a few moments of silence, Captain Gilroy said, "So, you're going up to see Arnold?"

"That's right. Do you know much about the situation up north?"

"All I know is that General Gates is now the Commander of the Northern Army, and that Arnold serves under him now. Are you well acquainted with General Arnold?"

"Never met him."

"Neither have I, but I've heard some things."

"Like what?"

"Well, what I've read in the papers. That he's a helluva commander of men. Smart, resourceful, and brave as Achilles."

"So I've heard."

"But I've also heard other things, passed down through the ranks. That he's only in it for the money."

"Well, I heard that he pays for food and equipment for his men right out of his own pocket," said Kinkaid, not liking where the conversation was going.

"I heard that, too," gave Captain Gilroy. "No, don't get me wrong, Lieutenant. I got nothing against Arnold. Don't even know the man. What I'm saying is that he's made a lot of enemies in the service, and there are officers, both high and low, that mean to drag him down. Why, a Major John Brown just published a handbill that accuses Arnold of all sorts of improprieties."

"Professional jealously, most likely," said Kinkaid, not one to besmirch a man's name with no proof, especially one who had proven himself in one fight after another and been wounded twice.

"I don't doubt that for a minute," said Captain Gilroy.

Wishing to change the subject, Kinkaid asked, "Can you give me a general idea of the route up to Glen's Falls from here?"

"Well, if you were on foot, I'd say just follow the deer trails along the river. But seeing as you've got wagons, you're gonna have to head west for a ways, around Bear Mountain. Even so, it's a damned rough trail and not easy on wagons, but you should manage if you're careful. You'll go through a rocky area and then you'll come to a better trail that leads down the hill, onto the flats. At the bottom you'll find a number of roads that converge. Don't take the first road to the right, but the second one. That will take you back to the road that more or less follows the river. If you leave early in the morning you should get back to the river by dusk. I haven't been any farther north than that, but that road should take you up to Glen's Falls."

"Well, I'm much obliged for that information, Captain."

Kinkaid wished that Sergeant Bowen had heard the description of the route as told by Captain Gilroy, but he would inform him of the directions in the morning.

Now it began to rain, and Captain Gilroy said, "You'd better have your men pitch your tents if you have 'em. Never know how hard it might rain tonight. We've had some earth-shaking thunder storms up here in the last week."

Kinkaid didn't have to roust the men, for Sergeant Bowen was already hauling their two tents out of the back of his wagon. The rain was just a light sprinkle at that point and it gave them plenty of time to set up the tents before it began to rain in earnest.

Kinkaid shared one of the tents with Sergeant Bowen, Corporal Sanderson and the two sailors, and at first the rain drummed loudly on the canvas, but then it just as quickly subsided into a light patter. With another day's riding behind him and a full stomach of bacon and beans, he was soon lulled into a deep sound sleep.

It was foggy the next morning because of the rain during the night, and because Kinkaid had only arrived at the army encampment as it was growing dark, he felt somewhat disoriented and had to ask Captain Gilroy the way to the road out while Sergeant Bowen was having their tents struck and packed into the back of his wagon.

"Just head up between those two oaks right up there," said Gilroy, pointing up the hill. "You'll find a big pine up there with a mark on it. Turn right there and that'll take you around Bear Mountain."

"Thank you, Captain."

"Just remember, when you get down the hill on the other side, don't take the first trail to the right. That road dead ends at a falls and a saw mill."

"I'm to take the second right," said Kinkaid, recalling Captain Gilroy's directions from the night before.

"That's right, Sir."

"Well, I wish you much luck here at this place and I hope the army hasn't forgotten about you and sends you some more supplies and men."

"I appreciate that, Lieutenant," said Gilroy, "and all the luck to you and your men wherever it is that General Arnold will be taking you."

The fog had burned off by the time they reached the rocky area that Captain Gilroy had mentioned, and the going was slow, with the men having to jump down from the wagons and pitch in and push and pull them over the rutted trail, and mostly uphill, at that. There were numerous cypress bogs on both sides of the road, and as if working up a sweat in the deep woods where there was scarcely a breeze wasn't bad enough, they were attacked by clouds of mosquitos that bit and stung them right through their shirts.

"I thought our mosquitos up in the Maine woods were bad," said Private Watkins, swatting frantically at a horde of them around his head with his hat. "But this cloud is thicker than hickory smoke. And hell, look at my ears. They bit me so much on my ears that they're twice the normal size."

"Which should give you double the hearing ability of the average man," said Sergeant Bowen, never one to pass up a good joke as long it was at another man's expense.

Private Watkins' ears were outlandishly swollen, which didn't help his looks one bit, for he'd never been handsome and his hair was like bristly wire. His worse feature, however, remained the perpetual scowl on his face.

"I had a friend who got bit so bad on his eyelids by black flies that they swelled up and he couldn't see for a week," said Private McDuff, a tall skinny red head.

"Hell, this ain't bad," said Private Metcalf. "At least you can see through 'em."

"That's right," said McDuff. "We got mosquitos up in the Maine woods that'll fly off with your cat or dog."

Not to be outdone, Metcalf said, "Why, that ain't nothin', We got skeeters so thick up in Vermont that you'd think they was cannonballs comin' at ya."

"Mosquitos thick as cannonballs? Now, that's a new one

on me," said Private McDuff, slapping his neck. "And all I can say is my eye, and what the hell, my leg, too."

"Well, they're liable to take yer eye and yer leg both before you knew you was missin' 'em."

"You men quit yer jawin' and get behind that wagon wheel," said Sergeant Bowen when his left front wheel slammed into another deep rut, adding, "This road ain't meant for wagons, Lieutenant."

"But it's the only road we've got, Sergeant."

"I don't know. I think Captain Gilroy sent us the wrong way. We're miles from the river by now."

"I know that, Sergeant, but we need to skirt around Bear Mountain first."

"According to Captain Gilroy. I just hope we don't break an axle."

"Just take your time and make sure we don't."

"Damn, what I wouldn't give for a beer right now."

"You and me, both, Sarg," said the skinny Metcalf, pulling on the wheel with all his might, to little effect until three other men helped him lift it out of the rut.

The wagon rolled for ten more feet before the same wheel slammed into an even deeper rut, taking six men to help lift it out this time.

"How far did you say it was to General Arnold's camp, Sarg?" asked Metcalf.

"Oh, about two hundred miles, give or take."

"Well, at this pace I'd say we might get there next summer."

"If the skeeters don't eat us first," said Private Watkins.

"It's not the skeeters that bother me as much as these damned ruts in the road, Sarg."

"What's a rut among friends?" asked Private McDuff.

"Hey, look," said Watkins, "the skeeters aren't biting

Metcalf."

They all turned to look at Metcalf, and sure enough, not only were the mosquitos not landing on him or biting him, but there wasn't a mosquito within five feet of Metcalf, much less a cloud of them.

"What the hell?" asked McDuff.

"It's his smell," said Watkins.

"Metcalf doesn't have a smell. He has a stink," said McDuff.

"I stand corrected."

"Shush up, boys," said Sergeant Bowen, stopping the wagon.

"What is it, Sarg?"

"I heard something up ahead."

Everyone stopped and listened, and sure enough, they all could hear a rustling of leaves in the forest ahead.

"Most likely some deer or turkeys," said O'Toole.

"Most likely Indians," said Bowen, refusing to move his wagon forward.

"I'll ride ahead and see," said Kinkaid.

He rode slowly forward, so as not to spook whatever it was that was moving through the forest ahead of them, and he hadn't gone far when he heard the leaves rustle again and then saw the flashes of white tails disappear into a cypress bog.

"Deer," was all Kinkaid said when he came back.

"I told you it was deer," said O'Toole smugly. "If there's Indians around, you won't hear 'em."

Which only made Sergeant Bowen look around warily before he eased his wagon forward again.

The wagons bounced and jounced over the rough trail for about three miles before they met another road that seemed more traveled, the better road that Captain Gilroy said they would come to, and the one that led them down the mountain.

It was almost noon now and getting hot and so Kinkaid allowed the men a fifteen minute break after their backbreaking labor of pulling wagon wheels out of one rut after another.

"I hope this takes us back to the river," said Sergeant Bowen.

Kinkaid ignored the comment, finding that Captain Gilroy's description of the trail had been right on the mark so far.

It should have been easier going on the new trail down the mountain, except that the wagons had to be braked most of the way and at some places it was so steep that the men had to grab ahold of ropes tied to the back axles of the wagons to hold them back so the horses or oxen wouldn't be run over from behind, so it wasn't any easier at all, but hard on the leg and arm muscles, and nerve-wracking as well.

Therefore it came as some relief when the trail started to level out by late that afternoon. Kinkaid noticed that there were less pine trees and cypress bogs and more maples and oaks, showing they'd managed a considerable change in elevation.

They passed through an old apple orchard and then came to a large open meadow where tall grasses, Queen Anne's lace and goldenrod blew gently in the breeze, and that is where they found the first fork in the road, one turning to the right, the other going straight ahead.

"We need to turn right here, Lieutenant," said Sergeant Bowen.

"Captain Gilroy specifically told me that we should take the second trail to the right," said Kinkaid. "I believe this is the first one."

48

"No, he's wrong," insisted Bowen. "I know this trail like the back of my hand, Sir. Used to take feed up to Newburgh on this trail. If we turn right here it'll take us back to the river road."

"Well, Captain Gilroy said we should not take this road. He told me that it dead ends at a falls and a saw mill."

"No, there ain't no saw mill hereabouts, Lieutenant," said Bowen adamantly. "Never has been. If we keep going straight we're gonna end up in New Jersey, Sir, and a long way from the river. Waste at least a day."

"Well, what do you say I ride up a ways and see where it goes?" suggested Kinkaid.

"I say you'd just be wasting your time," said Bowen, "but you're in charge, Sir."

Kinkaid spurred the horse along the right fork and soon entered another old growth forest, thick with spruce and tall pine trees. It was dark and cool here and he trotted along so as to leave the clouds of mosquitos behind. He was also cognizant of his anger at Sergeant Bowen for probably wasting their time arguing about the route when Captain Gilroy seemed more than familiar with the roads around here.

He'd gone a mile or more and then started to see the river through the trees. He was starting to think that perhaps this trail would take them back to the river road, starting doubting Captain Gilroy, when the Indian stepped out onto the trail not thirty yards in front of him, causing his horse to rear up.

The Indian just stood there as Kinkaid reined in and waited for his horse to calm down. Then he nudged her forward and the Indian said, "You go wrong way. This road ends at falls."

"That's what I was told."

"Then why you come this way?"

It was a reasonable question, though exasperating, and Kinkaid could only say, "We had a disagreement over the route."

"Who in charge?"

"Well, I am."

"Then why you allow disagreement?"

Before Kinkaid could think of a response the Indian said, "I think I come with you. Show you right way to Arnold's camp."

It was disconcerting, hearing the sensible advice from this Indian, but Kinkaid had to ask, "If this is the wrong way, then why are you here?"

"Short cut for me," he answered without hesitation. "I come over mountain; go through army camp, then follow deer trail along river to here."

"Those soldiers didn't see you?"

"Ha, you make Indian laugh."

"Jump up on back," said Kinkaid.

"No. I run."

The Indian gave a short whistle and the brown dog leaped out of the brush ahead of them, and then off they went, the Indian and his dog leading Kinkaid back the way he'd come, and at a pretty good pace, too, almost at a lope.

As they approached the fork Kinkaid thought at first that he'd better take the lead, but then changed his mind, thinking he would enjoy the look of shock on Sergeant Bowen's face.

He wasn't disappointed, for when Sergeant Bowen saw the Indian and the brown dog leading Kinkaid back his eyes looked ready to pop out of his head and his mouth hung open in disbelief.

"Catching mosquitos, Sergeant?" asked Kinkaid.

Sergeant Bowen snapped his mouth shut and asked, "What about the trail, Sir?"

"It's the wrong one. It took me to a dead end where there was a falls and a saw mill," he lied.

"Well, I don't understand that. I never heard of no saw mill around these parts."

"Must be a new trail…to a new saw mill. We'll take the next road to the right."

It was with some anxiety that Kinkaid led them straight ahead, with the Indian jogging some ways ahead of him, hoping that he'd made the right decision, and thinking that he probably should have followed the right fork a little farther, just to make sure it really did dead end at a falls and a saw mill.

But after about three miles they came to another fork in the road, and this time the Indian led them to the right and Sergeant Bowen didn't even argue about it. Two miles farther and they started seeing the river shining through the trees, and just as the light began to fade they found the road along the river where they camped for the night. Just like Captain Gilroy said they would.

Sergeant Bowen was unusually quiet that night around the campfire, especially after Kinkaid gave the red man a large pouch of tobacco.

IV

Something to Consider

The Indian kept to himself at his own small fire at the edge of their encampment, cooking his own meal, and the next morning he and his big brown dog were jogging out ahead of their group.

It turned out to be another perfect summer day, with pure white cottony clouds floating overhead, and with enough of a breeze to keep the temperature down. The road along the river was easy on the wagons, and the men were in good spirits.

All except for Sergeant Bowen, that is, who sat on his wagon mumbling and grumbling to himself, since Corporal Sanderson was too busy reading a book to pay much attention to what he had to say.

Corporal Sanderson had been diligently keeping a succinct and factual account of the group's progress and daily occurrences in a small booklet, but that didn't take much more than a half hour of his time, usually after dinner each evening, and so he had taken up the habit of reading as he rode beside the Sergeant, not only because he enjoyed reading, but he found that it kept Sergeant Bowen from pestering him with his foolish ideas and stories of his adventures and misadventures, most of them filled with gross exaggerations if not outright lies. Even the novel he was reading now, Robinson Crusoe, was more believable than the tall tales told by Sergeant Bowen, and his view of Indians was downright deplorable, in Sanderson's opinion.

They made good time and after passing numerous scattered farms they arrived at the small village of Newburgh around noon where Sergeant Bowen asked Kinkaid if they might stop and have a beer at the Red Stag Tavern.

"Very well," said Kinkaid, thinking the men had worked hard at getting the wagons around Bear Mountain and deserved a beer. "We shall stop for a pint, then. But no more than one per man, and I want to be back on the road in half an hour."

Kinkaid took a moment to check on the equipment in the back of Sergeant Bowen's wagon, since some pots and pans had fallen out of their sack that morning and had been making more noise than was necessary out on the trail.

There were only two men in the Red Stag Tavern, besides the keeper. Both were well-dressed lawyers, and neither seemed pleased when the dirty soldiers barged into their local watering hole and elbowed them aside at the bar.

"Let's take the corner table," suggested the tall one.

"Anything to get away from this rabble," said the short one.

"Pints all around!" boomed Sergeant Bowen, "and I'll take that big stein there."

"That stein belongs to the mayor," said the tavern keeper, a man as stout as Sergeant Bowen.

"Is the mayor here?" asked Bowen.

"He runs a farm and usually doesn't come in until after five."

"Well, then, you should be able to rinse it out and have it

ready for him by then."

"I'm sorry, but nobody touches the mayor's stein."

"Nobody touches the mayor's stein," mimicked Bowen like an eight-year old. "Well, then fill up your largest mug."

"All my mugs are the same size," said the man, placing a mug in front of Bowen.

Bowen took a sip, and then gulped down the whole pint before slamming the mug on the counter.

"Another!"

"The Lieutenant said one pint per man," Corporal Sanderson reminded him.

"Well, one beer for the average-sized man is the same as two beers for me."

The tavern keeper was in the process of refilling Sergeant Bowen's mug when Kinkaid came in.

"I made sure every man had a pint before I ordered my own," lied Bowen as the tavern keeper slid his second beer in front of him. "But you're welcome to this one, Sir."

Kinkaid noticed Corporal Sanderson rolling his eyes at what the sergeant had said, but it was the foam on Sergeant Bowen's upper lip that gave him away.

"No, go ahead, Sergeant. I can order my own. A pint, if you please."

"Coming right up, Sir."

As Kinkaid took a sip the tavern keeper asked him, "I don't recognize your uniform, Sir."

"Continental Navy."

"You don't say? Well, I have a brother in the Navy," said the man. "He's down in Philadelphia, aboard some frigate down there. A new ship, he says."

"Probably the *Randolph*," said Kinkaid.

"I do believe that is her name."

"A fine new design, from what I hear."

"Is that right?"

"That's right," said O'Toole. "She's a new design by Joshua Humphreys, and built for speed."

"I hope so, because if they go against those British ships, well…"

"Worried about your brother?" asked Jack Parker.

"A mite."

"I wouldn't be too worried. I heard that Nicholas Biddle is her commander. He's one of our best."

"He was captain of the *Franklin* and then the *Andrew Doria*," said O'Toole, "and has a good record."

"Well, that is good to hear and eases my mind somewhat."

"Where are you fellas headed?"

"Up to Lake Champlain, to join with General Arnold."

"I heard they're looking for carpenters."

"Carpenters, ship-builders, blacksmiths, almost any trade is needed."

"Another round, gentlemen?"

"I don't believe so," said Kinkaid.

"How about a pint on the house for our military men?" said the tavern keeper, raising his eyebrows and Sergeant Bowen's hopes.

"Thank you, and I appreciate the sentiment, good sir, but we need to get back on the road."

They'd all had their pint and Kinkaid was wary of questions coming from the strange tavern keeper who seemed full of questions and was apparently willing to expend his profits in an attempt to loosen their tongues some more.

"Not even one more, Sir?" asked Sergeant Bowen. "On the house?"

"Outside, Sergeant Bowen," said Kinkaid firmly.

Bowen snorted indignantly, but shuffled out, followed by

all the others, and they all climbed back up onto their respective wagons and were soon heading toward the outskirts of the town where the Indian and his dog were waiting for them.

It turned out to be an uneventful day, except that Private Metcalf shot a deer right from the top of the wagon that was standing in a field about a hundred feet from the road, which proved at least that Metcalf was a pretty good shot, and they stopped long enough to gut it and strip the hide that Metcalf insisted he keep. Metcalf even gave some of the meat to the Indian, but refused to give him the hide when he asked for it.

The Indian did go over to the head of the deer and chop the skull open. Then, after mashing the brain into a soupy pulp he packed the mess into a small leather pouch that hung on is belt while his dog made a meal of the deer's guts.

Sergeant Bowen had watched the Indian gather the deer brains and said, "Probably gonna drink that when he gets thirsty."

Metcalf added, "I heard they prefer it to ale."

"He probably believes it'll make him smart as a deer."

"Who are about twice as smart as your average Injin."

Both had a good laugh over that.

That evening they made camp near the tiny village of Esopus and while Private Watkins was frying up some venison steaks with wild onions that O'Toole had collected along the way, Kinkaid said, "O'Toole, I'd like you to invite the Indian to have supper with us."

"I suppose it don't hurt to ask, Sir."

O'Toole went over to where the Indian had his little fire and when he returned he said, "Just like I thought, Sir. He says he appreciates the invite, but he prefers to invite you to his fire, if you don't mind. He also told me he don't like to speak English, so you're gonna need me to translate, Sir."

"But he spoke English with me before. He speaks perfectly good English."

"I know, Sir. But that was only because he was alone with you and had no choice."

"What did you say the man's name was?"

"Well, it's kind of complicated, Sir. Something like Man Who Left the Bright Sunlight and by His Misfortune Went Under a Dark Cloud. He says General Arnold calls him Captain Cloud."

"I see. Well, let's go over."

The Indian stood up and offered them seats on a log that he'd drawn up next to his fire pit. And then he offered them some of his venison stew that he had bubbling in a little pot over the fire. The dog sat off to the side and paid little attention to them, gnawing on the bones of a woodchuck it had killed.

Kinkaid was too polite to refuse the Indian stew and when he brought the first spoonful up to his mouth with some trepidation he was not prepared for how delicious it tasted.

"Tell him this is very good."

O'Toole didn't need to translate what Kinkaid said, for the Indian understood him perfectly, and he spoke in his Indian tongue for some time before O'Toole translated.

"He says he already knows how good his stew is, Sir. He says he stole some potatoes and carrots at some farm in Newburgh and then collected some wild onions along the road that gives it that extra kick. He also says that he hopes you are not insulted by him not wanting to come to your fire, and explains that he doesn't trust most white men until he gets to know them. He calls his dog Little Scout, and says he doesn't trust white men either."

"Well, I can understand that."

The Indian merely grunted at that and then the three of

them sat there and ate in silence.

Afterwards the Indian brought out his pipe, packed it, got it going, and then passed it to Kinkaid.

Not being a smoker, Kinkaid took the pipe and puffed on it but was careful not to inhale and choke, thinking it might be taken as an insult, before passing it back to the Indian who offered it to O'Toole.

But O'Toole took out his own fancy carved pipe and smoked from his own bowl, whereupon O'Toole and the Indian started talking.

Finally, O'Toole said, "He recognized my pipe as coming from one of the Narragansett tribes, Sir. He remembers when he was a young man and they used to go raiding there. Says they have some fine looking women, some of which they stole from them. But now he is sad that so many of those people are gone now, and hopes the Iroquois don't meet the same fate, but says he has bad dreams concerning his people in that regard."

"What was the fate of those Indians?"

"Well, first they were ravaged by white men's diseases. And then the white men started stealing their land. And then the missionaries came and tried to stop them from being Indians. Should I go on, Sir?"

"I think I get the picture. Ask him why he works for General Arnold?"

"He says it's that white missionary's fault; Kirkland, who lived among his people for many years and tricked them into believing in the white man's god. Says he only works for Arnold because of the money he's paid, not because he believes in our cause. And if it comes to a fight, he said he would refuse to kill his brothers.

"His brothers?"

"Of the other Iroquois tribes."

"I see. Well, I can't blame him for..." Kinkaid looked the Indian in the eye and said, "I can't blame you for that. And I admire your honesty."

Now the Indian said in English, "Man who lies has no honor."

They sat in front of the fire for some time before the Indian spoke again.

"He wants to know if he can have the skin of the deer we shot today; says the nights are getting chilly with the coming of fall and he needs a new buckskin shirt."

"Well, I'd have to ask Private Metcalf about that."

The Indian grunted in disgust at Kinkaid's answer, pointed at Kinkaid and said, "White officer need to learn to be stronger leader."

Kinkaid's first impulse was to take offense, but then he said, "I will consider your words."

After all, the Indian had a point. Kinkaid had not led much of anything yet, and knew he was too concerned about men liking him. In fact, even with this bunch of ten that he was in charge of, he was reluctant to give them orders, felt uncertain of holding his rank over them. The Indian's opinion was certainly something to consider.

They were packed up and back on the road by sunup and that is when Kinkaid rode alongside Sergeant Bowen's wagon.

He'd been thinking about how he might approach Private Metcalf about giving the deer hide to the Indian when he immediately realized that Metcalf would never go for the idea, especially knowing that Sergeant Bowen held such a low opinion of Indians and that Private Metcalf followed after Bowen like a whipped mongrel. But Kinkaid also did not feel comfortable with ordering Metcalf to give the hide to the Indian, realizing that soldiers today, especially since the signing of the Declaration of Independence, possessed a newfound regard for the notion of freedom. Why, most militia officers these days were even voted into their position by the soldiers under them. That left only one solution.

"Private Metcalf, what were you thinking you'd do with that deer hide?"

"I thought I might sell it when we got to Albany, Sir."

"And how much would you expect to get for it?"

"Oh, seein' as it ain't properly cured, I'd say it's worth at least six shillings."

"I'll give you twelve shillings for it."

"Well, that's right generous of you, Sir, and you got yourself a deal!"

And that is how Kinkaid managed to give Metcalf's deer hide to the Indian, who rolled it up and tucked it into his parfleche without as much as a thank you.

Later that evening the Indian had the hide unrolled by his campfire and could be seen scrapping the hair off with a skinning knife and flint scrapper. He worked on it for hours until it was completely hairless, and then he took that pouch off his belt with the scrambled deer brains in it and rubbed and worked the mess into the hide.

O'Toole noticed Kinkaid watching the man at his labor and said, "Deer brains will make that hide as soft and smooth as a baby's behind, Sir."

The next evening found the Indian cutting the hide into three pieces and then he had them sewed together in a couple of hours.

The next day the Indian was seen jogging out ahead of them in his brand new deerskin shirt, yellowish-white and bright as could be, and the sight of it stirred the wrath and envy of Sergeant Bowen and Private Metcalf to the point where they could be heard muttering to each other about, "murderin' Injins and their heathen ways."

Kinkaid could only imagine what the two of them thought of him, buying Metcalf's deerskin at double the price he would have asked for it in Albany and then giving it to the Indian for free so he could have a clean new shirt.

But then Kinkaid was his own man and their leader and he didn't really care what Sergeant Bowen or Private Metcalf thought of him, and he looked forward to the day when they would arrive at Fort Ticonderoga and Bowen would be put to work as a blacksmith while Kinkaid went off with General Arnold. Actually, the idea that those two might have their sensibilities roiled by what he had done put a smile on his face as he rode along behind the Indian called Captain Cloud and his dog, Little Scout.

V

The Enemy is About

It was almost two in the afternoon by the time they reached Albany, and Kinkaid was of a mind to push right on through without stopping, one reason being that he had heard that the citizens of Albany tended to be Tories who valued money over patriotism and he'd as soon not mingle with them.

But when Sergeant Bowen noticed that they were passing a dilapidated shack with a sign over the door that read, The Boar's Head, he couldn't stop himself from shouting, "Aren't you gonna let us stop for a pint, Lieutenant?"

"Not today, Sergeant. I have an appointment with General Arnold and I have no intention of being late, so I believe we'll push right on through."

Sergeant Bowen didn't say a word but he did take his hat off and slap it on his knee with some force, showing that he was downright distressed by having to pass up a chance to whet his whistle and disgusted with Kinkaid's unreasonable decision.

Albany was a fair-sized town, and laid out in neat blocks of homes and businesses and nobody paid much attention to the two wagons with ten men piled on top as they passed through, being accustomed to seeing plenty of wagons and soldiers and all manner of frontiersmen come through, especially since the war broke out, and probably one of the reasons that many of her upstanding citizens were Tories was that they were afraid the war would come their way and disrupt their business.

But that didn't mean it wasn't nice to see some pretty girls again as they passed through, walking around in their pretty dresses, since most of the scenery they'd seen so far was bereft of pretty girls, and all they'd seen so far of civilization were some run down farms and a few grungy men working their fields.

As they approached the northern outskirts they noticed some groups of soldiers and then saw a few dozen tents set up in neat rows along the road where a regiment of Continentals were encamped.

They were almost past the last few tents when someone shouted, "Hey, you men with those wagons!"

Kinkaid turned in his saddle to see who had shouted and saw that some officer was running up behind them, all red in the face.

"Who are you and where are you going with those supplies?" asked the officer, a colonel by the red cockade on his hat.

"Lieutenant Kinkaid, of the Continental Navy, going up to join with General Arnold, Sir," answered Kinkaid.

"Are you now? I heard they were sending some navy people up. Are you from here in Albany?"

"No, Sir, I'm from Boston. I met with the others at Tappan Zee, and well, I'm not sure where they're all from."

"The reason I ask is that the shipyard here is sending men up to Arnold, too. Well, we're going up there, as well, and you should join with us."

"Sir, I have strict orders to see General Arnold without delay and…"

"I am Colonel Lucas of the 3rd Connecticut Volunteers from Windham and Hartford counties, and I must insist that you and your wagons join with our party…it's for you own protection and the security of those supplies."

"Well, Sir…"

"In fact, I order you to join us."

What could Kinkaid do? He had been given a direct order by a higher ranking officer, and as an officer himself in his country's service, he was expected to obey orders as well as give them.

"Very well, Sir, I must comply then, but I should apprise you of the fact that I have been instructed to report to General Arnold with all due haste."

"Just give my people time to strike our tents and we shall be on the road within the hour. We would have been on the road by now but for the procurement of some beef that will be much appreciated by General Arnold's command. You will join my baggage train as it comes through."

And so they sat there on the road while Colonel Lucas's 3rd Connecticut Regiment struck their tents, then packed up and formed up.

In the meantime, Private Watkins put the time to good use by going out in a corn field on the opposite side of the road and collecting about six dozen ears of ripe corn.

By the time Watkins had all that corn stashed in the back of their wagon, the 3rd Connecticut Regimen came marching down the road in a column of twos, followed by a couple of small bore howitzers. Behind them came Lucas's baggage train with half a dozen wagons, piled with all manner of supplies as well as women and children and following along behind all that was a small herd of cattle.

It was dusty, riding behind the marching columns of men and their baggage train, and noisy, too, with a dozen children running alongside their wagons, shouting and hollering, "Look, there's an Injin!"

But Captain Cloud had no intention of being gawked and goggled over by some white brats and he soon disappeared into the forest along with his dog, and Kinkaid couldn't really blame him.

"That's the last we'll see of him," observed O'Toole.

It was an unwelcome development as far as Kinkaid was concerned, to have to join this contingent. Not only did it take away his autonomy, but it seemed to diminish the small amount of authority he was beginning to enjoy. Although all those soldiers looked impressive marching along with their muskets on their shoulders, and they marched along at a reasonable pace and did not slow his wagons appreciably, he knew that a group this size would take much longer to set up camp and strike again the next day.

As if aware of Kinkaid's apprehensions, Colonel Lucas soon rode up beside him with his aide-de-camp and said, "I should say that I am glad to have you with us, Lieutenant, and I hope you will not be inconvenienced by joining with us, but I must remind you that the enemy is about, not to mention bandits who would be glad to relieve you of your stores and equipment, and you will be safer with us."

"It is the delay that concerns me, Colonel."

"Of course, and I understand that, but let me assure you that we are normally on the road by sunup and besides, we are only five or six days from Arnold's camp and I must bring your attention to the fact that it will be better to arrive a few hours late than not to arrive at all or have to tell General Arnold that his supplies and equipment were stolen. Furthermore, I will take full responsibility for any delay we might cause you, Sir, should General Arnold make an issue of the matter."

Colonel Lucas was doing his best to make the situation acceptable to Kinkaid, but after all he had his concerns and was a senior officer and didn't have to say a word to justify any order he might give, yet he had gone out of his way to do so and Kinkaid had to respect that.

"I appreciate your concern, Colonel."

"Good. We'll talk some more when I make my rounds tonight," said the Colonel before he rode off to make sure all the cattle he'd acquired in Albany was following in good order.

A light rain fell on the column most of that afternoon, making for a cool march and keeping the dust down as well, and that evening Private Watkins cooked up a very delicious corn chowder. But then Kinkaid was finding that almost any meal cooked and devoured around a campfire out in the fresh air, and especially after a long, hard day on the trail, always tasted inordinately good.

Kinkaid also had a chance to learn more about the men under his command as he overheard them conversing while they ate their evening meal around the campfire.

"Hell, I was gonna become a Presbyterian minister before all this," said Corporal Sanderson. "But I figured saving my country was akin to saving souls, and so here I am. What about you Watkins? Did your master send you into this army so he wouldn't have to go himself?"

Watkins crinkled up his dark brow and in a low, sad voice said, "No, my master died two years ago and I was set free upon his passing; God bless ole Mister Crabb. Left me a bit of money, too, and I had the chance to be a partner in a tavern and inn venture over near Danbury. But then my partner got drunk and gambled his share of our investment away. Left me stuck in the lurch, so I joined up. But I'll get that inn someday, and when I do I aim to marry little Annie Rowland over in Fairfield. She makes the best apple pie in the county."

"Well, that's a mighty nice compliment to your future bride, Watkins, and a good pie is an asset to any establishment catering to the public," said Sanderson, giving Able Seaman Jack Parker a knowing wink.

"Well, she's pretty, too, in her own way," said Watkins in defense, a man who would never win a beauty contest.

"And a right lucky lass to snag a handsome lad like yourself," said Parker, returning Sanderson's wink.

"And jovial, too," threw in McDuff, joining in the ribbing.

"I know I ain't no prize," admitted Watkins, "but I can cook better'n most and aim to be a good provider."

"And not many can say that," gave Sanderson. "What about you, Jack, what were you doing before the war?"

"Well, first I worked on my father's fishing boat," said Jack. "But then the creditors took our boat and so I signed on to the *Unity*, a privateer out of Newport. That's where I met Boats, here."

"That's right," said O'Toole. "We got lucky, too, and took eight prizes before we was cornered by a couple of English frigates in the Sound. Had to burn her, God help us. That's when me and Jack signed up for the navy and they sent us up here, thinking we'd be useful, and not having nothing else available."

"Well, I don't know that I'd like to be on a Continental Navy ship these days, not up against the Royal Navy. Why, it seems like suicide."

"Perhaps our luck still holds, Jack," said O'Toole with a grin.

Colonel Lucas stopped by their fireplace after supper and

had a word with Kinkaid.

"I'm one of two regiments under General Waterbury," explained Lucas. "The General is with the other regiment and is a day ahead of us since he detached us to acquire that herd of cattle in Albany today. We're going up to reinforce Arnold."

"What do you know of the situation up north, Colonel?"

"Well, I know that the British have forced our retreat from Montreal, but that we still hold Crown Point and Ticonderoga, thanks to Arnold. And now the British will have to build a fleet to take them down Lake Champlain since there are no roads to speak of and they can't get their ships down the Richelieu, and I believe that is how Arnold hopes to delay them…with a fleet of his own. But I also heard that smallpox has decimated the ranks of our northern army and that Gates and Arnold is in dire need of both reinforcements and carpenters. Are your men carpenters?"

"Uh, yes, some of them," answered Kinkaid uncertainly, having only Sergeant Bowen's word on the matter.

"Well, then they will be welcomed by Arnold. Good carpenters are hard to come by these days. We were tasked with recruiting as many ship's carpenters as we could find before we left Connecticut but couldn't get but half a dozen. Do you know they're all lucratively employed in the building of privateer vessels? Why, ever since they passed that privateering resolution in March every ship's captain in New England thinks he's going to get rich from this war by taking British merchant ships…as if the British Navy won't have any say in the matter."

"Then they're in for a rude awakening," said Kinkaid.

"And where in the world do they expect to get cannons?"

"Many will resort to fakery, I'm afraid."

"I heard about that tactic; using logs to look like guns."

"They refer to them as Quakers, Colonel," said Kinkaid, shaking his head.

"Well, good luck to them is all I can say. What is the extent of your service thus far, Lieutenant, if you don't mind my asking?"

"I began my service as a cabin boy aboard the armed sloop *Vesper* in '74, and then as a gunnery officer aboard the brig *Aries*, all this before the Navy was formed and I was commissioned, that is."

"Of course. Now, the *Vesper*; that name rings familiar for some reason. She is known for something, but what it is escapes me now."

"You probably read about her captain in the newspapers," said Kinkaid, reluctantly recalling the dreaded memory of those days. "She was commanded by a Captain Davenport…who killed a fellow officer."

"Ah, yes…and was cleared of all charges as I recall."

"Yes. Yes, he was," said Kinkaid, remembering the man who had been killed, a good and able lieutenant by the name of James O'Neil, a man who had gone out of his way to make life a little less miserable for a young and naïve midshipman unlucky enough to have been sent aboard a ship commanded by the sadistic Captain Davenport.

"Well, he must have had a good reason, then."

"I suppose," was all Kinkaid could say, knowing very well that Captain Davenport had murdered Lieutenant O'Neil in a fit of rage and then had bullied and threatened the other ship's officers into testifying on his behalf, had terrorized them into lying and saying that Davenport had only acted in self-defense, ensuring a favorable judgment from the court of inquiry.

Suspecting from Kinkaid's response that the matter brought up unpleasant memories, Lucas asked, "So you're going up to join Arnold's fleet. Now what kind of a fleet does Arnold hope to build in a few months? I can only imagine that the building of even a single ship must be a major undertaking."

"I'm eager to ascertain that myself, Colonel. I understand he already had two schooners and a sloop and can only guess that he means to add a number of gunboats of some type."

"Well, we're only a few days away from his camp, so I suppose we'll soon…"

Their conversation was interrupted by an officer rushing toward them between campfires and shouting, "Colonel!"

"What is it, Major Warren?" asked Colonel Lucas, standing up.

"Indian attack, Sir, on the north side of the camp," said the man breathlessly. "A group of six went into the woods and were attacked. Two killed and two wounded."

"How many Indians were there?"

"Hard to tell, Sir. One man said a dozen, another said upwards of thirty."

"Take me to them, Major. Care to accompany me, Lieutenant?"

"Of course, Colonel," said Kinkaid, for when a colonel asks you to do something you don't say no.

They had to go through the entire camp first, which meant skirting numerous campfires that stung the eyes and assaulted the nostrils with the smell of beans and bacon, and it was some time before they reached the northernmost edge of the encampment where two dozen men were standing with muskets in their hands, bayonets fixed. Others held blazing firebrands that lit up the area around them.

"This is Captain Moore, Sir," said Major Warren. "They were in his company."

"I'm sorry about your men, Captain, but we'll have to be more careful in the future."

"Yes, Sir."

"Where are they?"

"Right this way, Colonel."

"I don't want any surprises, Captain."

"I have my entire company surrounding the area, Sir."

"Very well. Let's go, then."

Captain Moore took one of the blazing firebrands and led them through some thick brush that they all stumbled through before the forest opened to larger trees and open glades. Then they came to the edge of another one of those spruce bogs that seemed to be so prevalent in the north woods.

It was the smell that hit Kinkaid first, and then the sound of flies buzzing.

"Here is the first one, Sir," said Captain Moore, pointing to a pool of stagnant water where an indistinct form lay. "Looks like he thought to escape in the swamp but got caught in the mud."

Colonel Lucas went over to the spot that Captain Moore was illuminating. He looked down and said, "You might want to have a look at this, Lieutenant."

Kinkaid reluctantly stepped forward until he saw the form lying there on his back in the mud. The man was stark naked and seemed to glow an unnatural grayish color in the flickering light. His body was covered in bloody hack marks, obviously made by knives and tomahawks, and his genitals had been hacked off and stuffed into his mouth. His scalp had also been taken and his face was covered in blood, the eyes open, staring vacantly into the night sky. They had more than killed the man. It was a gruesome sight and Kinkaid found himself taking a deep breath and fighting the urge to vomit.

"The other is over here," said Captain Moore, stepping behind a small copse of saplings.

"I've seen enough, Captain," said the colonel. "What were these men doing out here, Captain?"

"Collecting firewood."

"And about how many Indians were there?"

"I'm not sure, Sir, but it seems at least a dozen. We weren't even aware of anything until it was all over."

"Of course not. They used knives and tomahawks so as not to arouse the camp."

"It appears so, Sir. I heard no discharge of firearms."

"Well, let's take these men back to camp. We'll bury them in the morning with full military honors. See to the proper protocol, will you, Major Warren?"

"Of course, Colonel."

"How are your wounded faring, Captain?"

"One man has a nasty gash on his arm, but the other took a tomahawk to his face, Sir. It crushed his cheek and severed an eye. He is presently in a coma."

"Probably better for him that he is. But rest assured, Captain, that my surgeon shall provide him the best of care."

"Thank you, Sir."

Kinkaid learned the next morning that the wounded man had died during the night, bringing the total to three killed.

By the time the men were given a military funeral and buried, the news had spread about the camp that the dead men had had their genitals cut off and stuffed into their mouths, as well as been scalped and suffered other mutilations. There was also a rumor to the effect that the attacking force numbered over thirty warriors, all of these facts and rumors repeated over and over again by Sergeant Bowen who swore that he would, "get some revenge on those murderin' savages the first chance I get."

It seemed that the entire army was on alert as they passed through a vast forest that day, a dark and gloomy place, hiding god knows what, and many could imagine red-painted faces and evil and blood-thirsty eyes watching them from the pine trees and spruce bogs as they passed.

That evening Colonel Lucas stopped by and told Kinkaid, "I've posted more sentries, and those men detailed to gather firewood or tend to the horses or the cattle have been provided strong security details. Just ensure that your men follow proper precautions if they need to leave the camp for any reason. I shall also send out patrols every morning as well as provide a company of skirmishers to lead our advance in order to protect us from possible ambuscade."

"I appreciate the warning, Colonel," said Kinkaid. "And I must thank you for insisting that we join your column, Sir, for if not for you stopping us…"

"As I mentioned, Lieutenant, the enemy is about, and they are employing the savage to conduct their scouting and hit and run tactics for them. But a good show of force should keep them at bay."

The incident was Kinkaid's first up front and personal taste of the war. It was no longer something that he only read about in the papers, but was real, and he would never forget the sight of that poor man lying there, hacked up and brutalized the way he was. It was suddenly a very dangerous world where men would die. And to think that his career and his life might have been cut short if he and his small group had gone on alone, that they might have suffered the same fate if not for Colonel Lucas ordering him to join their column... Well, the thought gave him a chill up his spine.

The next day was another one of those beautiful late summer days as the column left the Hudson River, only a small stream now and a shadow of her former glory, as the bank turned toward the west where it ran down from the Adirondack Mountains, and after another day of travel over a muddy trail they arrived at the shore of Lake George.

VI

Fort Ticonderoga

Lake George was the first real lake they had come to, and though it was a rather large lake, it didn't seem big enough to hold a fleet of ships, thought Kinkaid as he gazed out over its calm shimmering waters. Even so, it was nice to see the open expanse of the sky over the lake where a couple of bald eagles were soaring, especially after the gloom of the forest they had just passed through.

There was a fort there too, called Fort George, and Sergeant Bowen made the astute observation, "Somebody must have racked his brains to come up with that name," as they passed by its sloped stone walls.

And that brought from Private Metcalf, "Especially since they named the lake George, too," and everybody had a good laugh over that; everybody except Private Metcalf who just scratched his head and couldn't understand what was so funny.

But they didn't even look inside the fort that now served more as a supply depot and hospital, because Colonel Lucas kept his column moving right past the western blockhouse and headed them north up the trail that followed the western shoreline.

About halfway up the lake is where they found the now famous privateer captain David Hawley camping with over thirty Connecticut sailors that he had brought with him on their way up to join with Gates and Arnold, and the story began circulating about how he had escaped from a Halifax prison and rowed over five hundred miles in a week, back to American lines, and he too was ordered, along with his men, to join with Colonel Lucas's 3rd Connecticut Regiment for his own protection.

Actually, lake George seemed to get bigger and bigger as they hiked along its western shore, and when one of Hawley's sailors said they doubted there was a lake big enough for a fleet to sail on Colonel Lucas told them that Lake Champlain made Lake George look like a farm pond, and that is when Kinkaid first began to appreciate the idea of a fleet on a lake.

He could also appreciate the wild beauty of the area they were entering now, a place of vast forests and mountains that surrounded the lake, dotted with numerous islands covered in pine and spruce. It was the beginning of September now and the days were clear and the nights were cold, and the maples were already beginning to turn, with hints of yellow and gold and burnished red on the hillsides.

But the men remained nervous and vigilant after their encounter with that Indian raiding party that had taken three of their soldiers in the night, and it was the nights that had them jumping at shadows, in fear that an Indian lurked behind every tree.

Lake George was long and seemed to go on forever and it wasn't until the evening of the second day along its shore that they finally arrived at the northern end where Colonel Lucas' forward skirmishers ran into a patrol sent out from Fort Ticonderoga.

That patrol led the column over a series of wooden bridges that spanned a maze of waterways where the mountains seemed to squeeze the northern end of Lake George into the southern end of Lake Champlain, and after passing through a marshy swamp they finally came out at a narrow body of water that revealed the gray stone walls of the fort high up on a promontory, where the black snouts of heavy cannon poked through parapets and embrasures.

A steep mountain was to the left of where the fort sat, called Mount Defiance, and across the inlet was Mount Independence, now largely bereft of trees where a city of tents, cabins and lean-tos sat and where numerous campfires sent up plumes of dirty gray smoke.

But what caught Kinkaid's eyes was the cluster of docks along the shore under the fort where half a dozen boats were being fitted out. One was a good-sized schooner, another was a sloop, but most of them were light, flat-bottomed gundalos, usually employed as cargo vessels, but each one of these was armed with at least a single heavy cannon. One of the ships, however, looked unfamiliar to Kinkaid, especially with its lateen sails hanging sideways from two masts, a craft that Kinkaid had never seen before. Along the shoreline were at least a hundred or more whaleboats, bateaux and canoes all lined up in neat rows and turned upside down.

As they drew nearer they could see groups of men running back and forth from the docks and shacks along the shore to the boats and there were many other men aboard them; shipwrights, carpenters, blacksmiths, armorers and riggers, all swarming over the various vessels, all working frantically to prepare Arnold's fleet in time to stop the British, and it was pretty exciting to see all this frenzied activity.

Along the docks were stacked all manner of supplies and

equipment of all kinds, from brass carriage guns to piles of cannon balls and spars and heaps of cordage to barrels of salt pork and rum.

Now Kinkaid could hear all the shouting of those men, and when they noticed the column of troops coming their way they let out a cheer and it was a thrilling moment when the booms of cannons were heard from the fort in salute and they saw the white puffs of smoke drifting over the mountain high above.

"You'll want to report to General Gates at the fort, Colonel," said some captain to Colonel Lucas as they rode up. "Just bear off to the left there and that road will take you up."

"Very well, Captain," said Lucas and with that he spurred his horse and went riding up the road to the left, the one that wound up the hill to the fort.

"I was told to report to General Arnold, Captain," said Kinkaid. "Can you direct me to his camp?"

"General Arnold's camp? Well, General Arnold camps with his fleet now, Sir, aboard the *Royal Savage*, mostly, but I believe you'll find him down in Skenesboro today."

"And how would I get to Skenesboro?"

"Well, I wouldn't advise going down there. Everybody down there has come down with the ague."

Exasperated, Kinkaid asked, "Well, if I had to go down there, how would I do that?"

"The best way would be by boat."

"I don't have a boat."

"If you rode down you'd probably miss him. Either way you'd probably miss him as I doubt he'll stay down there very long."

"Do you know where he might be going then, after he leaves there?"

"No, I couldn't guess. I'd suggest you report in with General Gates. He'll know where to send you."

"Thank you, Captain."

Kinkaid then went over to where Sergeant Bowen still sat on his wagon.

Pointing to the activity along the shore, he said, "Sergeant Bowen, I need to report that we're all here. In the meantime, why don't you and your men pitch in and help those men with the fitting out of their ships and boats."

"I think we can do that, Lieutenant," said Sergeant Bowen, seeming agreeable for a change. The truth was that Sergeant Bowen looked forward to being able to give his men some practical and meaningful orders again, something he hadn't been able to do much while on the road.

"I should be back shortly and let you know where we're to make camp."

"Whatever you say, Lieutenant," said Bowen, jumping down from the wagon, glad to know that Kinkaid would be out of his hair for a while.

And now Kinkaid took the same road that Colonel Lucas had taken up to the fort, and it was a crowded trail, with patrols coming and going.

Long before he even got to the fort he had to pass through several guarded checkpoints where ditches had been dug and strong redoubts had been constructed at the top of the mountain, and he could see for miles over the surrounding countryside from up there because all the trees had been cleared away for two hundred yards around the fort, and it was some time before he arrived at the big iron-bound oak door where five sentries stood guard, and it wasn't until after they asked him the same questions the other strongpoints had asked him that they finally let him through the small door or wicket gate into the thick stone-walled fort at

Ticonderoga, newly rebuilt under General Arnold's orders and specifications.

First built in 1758 by the French, it had been named Fort Carillon then and successfully defended against the British General James Abercromby the year it was built, but then was abandoned the next year when General Jeffrey Amherst showed up with an overwhelming force. Since then it had fallen into decay until General Arnold arrived and ordered it repaired and better fortified.

Once inside the fort, Kinkaid was met by General Gate's aide de camp, a rather droll and overly serious man who introduced himself as Colonel Wilkinson who showed Kinkaid to a straight-backed chair just outside the General's office.

Kinkaid didn't know anything about Colonel Wilkinson; didn't know that Wilkinson had once been General Arnold's aide de camp, and that Arnold had fired him for drinking too much, and so now he had gotten himself hired as General Gate's aide de camp. He also didn't know that Wilkinson hated Arnold with a passion bordering on murder, just as most drunks hate those who point out their self-destructive obsession for alcohol, and Wilkinson took every opportunity to disparage General Arnold in front of General Gates whenever the opportunity presented itself. All this would have far reaching ramifications in the future, but at the time Kinkaid didn't give Wilkinson a thought as he sat there outside the General's office.

There wasn't much in the small anteroom to look at except for a pair of crossed sabers on the wall and a fireplace that looked like it had never been used, but at least it was cool and it wasn't that long before Wilkinson came back out of the door and said, "The General will see you now," whereupon Kinkaid was ushered in to see the Commanding

General of the Northern Army, General Horatio Gates.

"Lieutenant Jonathan Kinkaid of the Continental Navy reporting, Sir."

"Ah, another sailor," said Gates, standing up from his desk. He seemed to have a back problem and couldn't quite stand up straight, but he shook Kinkaid's hand firmly enough before he sat back down and said, "You must be the one came up with Colonel Lucas' Connecticut Volunteers today."

"That's right, Sir."

Gates was an old man, with gray hair and long scraggly gray whiskers along both sides of his face that could have used a good trimming. But he seemed friendly enough as he sat behind his desk that was piled high with letters and papers all in a jumble, and now he looked over his spectacles and asked, "How many sailors did you bring with you?"

"Only two, Sir," said Kinkaid, sounding to himself like a complete and utter fool. "But in addition to myself and an orderly I've also brought seven carpenters recruited from a New England militia regiment."

"Well, what we really need up here are some real sailors, but that's ten men in all, and ten men here and ten men there adds up, and carpenters are as good as gold," Gates said cordially enough. "I suppose you'll be looking for General Arnold."

"Yes, Sir."

"Well, I'll tell you the same thing I just told Colonel Lucas and Captain Hawley. Arnold is a hard one to pin down these days. One minute he's aboard one ship or boat or another and the next minute he's coming up and bothering me about shoes or coats or powder or nails, or else he's up on Mount Independence, checking on the progress of our fortifications up there. Right now I believe he's down in Skenesboro, looking over the last of his row galleys. That's where most of his shipbuilding is being done, you know. But I doubt he'll be down there for long before he's back up here, getting after those men who are already working their tails to the bone trying to finish fitting out his completed boats. We finish fitting them out up here, or else up at Crown Point. So I'd suggest you stay right here and let him come to you. Is there anything you or your men need in the meantime? The last of our beer ran out a week ago and I don't know when more will be sent up."

"Well, we could use some shoes and some clothing, Sir."

"Shoes and clothing. Well, other than beer those are about the most popular items on anybody's list around here. But they also happen to be the scarcest items, and I have to tell you that I don't rightly know when they'll be sending any shoes or clothing up. Hopefully soon because the weather is about to turn, but there's so much of everything else that we need that things like shoes and clothing seems to keep getting left off those supply wagons for some reason. And that reminds me that I should probably write another letter requesting more shoes and clothing, not that it'll do any good, but that seems to be my main job around here, writing letters for this and that. Say, did you happen to bring any cordage with you?"

"Ten or so coils, I believe."

"Any good duck canvas?"

"Some, as well as a good supply of sail needles and palms, spikes and nails, spun yarn, seizing, a couple barrels of oakum; I can make a list for you, Sir."

"No need for that. Just turn it over to a man named Gordy down at the docks; he'll find a use for everything you brought. In fact, you can't believe everything we need. From anchors and hawsers and rope of every size you can imagine, to blocks and pulleys, half-hour glasses, spyglasses, pots and pans, flags, pistols and cutlasses, speaking trumpets, fishing nets; you name it, we need it. Why, we need just about everything any shipyard needs, but are just about out of everything. Good thing we have plenty of paper and ink, at least. Now then, is there anything else I can do for you?"

"Where should we set up our camp?"

"Well, most of the outfits are over on Mount Independence, but it's getting a mite crowded over there now and firewood is getting scarce, so since there are only ten of you, I'd say go ahead and set up your camp wherever you can find room and wherever you're not in anybody's way."

General Gates seemed like a real fussbudget by the way he seemed to get caught up with every detail, thought Kinkaid, and he could see why they had nicknamed him "Granny" Gates.

"Well, thank you, Sir, for your help and advice. I'll wait for General Arnold to show up, then."

When Kinkaid returned down the hill he found Sergeant Bowen on the dock in front of that odd-looking craft he'd seen before, the one with the strange rig. Bowen was at the north end of a two-handled saw while Able Seaman Jack Parker worked the south end, and the two were sawing through a big beam being held steady by the rest of the boys, and there wasn't much room for them to work because stacked behind them were piles of cannonballs and about a dozen barrels of powder and practically under their feet was the massive barrel of an 18 pounder cannon. It occurred to Kinkaid as he watched the men work that meaningful activity seemed to be the antidote for Sergeant Bowen's otherwise shiftless character and desultory attitude.

Once the beam had been sawed to the proper length it was hoisted up and attached to another set of beams, forming a strong hoist, and now men scrambled around the huge 18-pounder cannon underneath, passing heavy hawsers under it and cinching them tight with expertly tied knots and then passing those lines through a couple of pulleys attached to the hoist.

Now a shipwright took charge and started shouting orders and all those men started hauling on the ropes and before long that massive 18-pounder was swinging in the air like a child's toy. They swung it out over the bow of the strange boat and then lowered it down onto its truck as gently as laying a baby in its crib.

"There's another one, Gordy!" shouted one of the men beside the newly installed cannon.

"Damn if I don't do good work," said the shipwright named Gordy.

"*We* do good work, Gordy," said another. "*We.*"

"That's right, Gordy, we earn our forty shillings a month," said another. "You just provide the jawbonin'"

"But I'm paid to jawbone, and you ain't, so shut your mouths and get those cannonballs aboard!"

The good-natured teasing was appreciated by all and even had Sergeant Bowen smiling as he wiped the sweat from his brow from their efforts, and now Gordy the shipwright came over and asked, "Who are you, boys?"

"We're up from Connecticut," said the sergeant. "All of us experienced carpenters. I'm Sergeant Bowen. I'm a blacksmith, as well, and am in charge of this group."

Gordy walked over to where Jack Parker stood while Bowen gave his speech and he said, "Where'd you get those muscles, son?" squeezing Parker's forearm.

"They just grew, Sir," said Parker, embarrassed and at a loss for words.

"Well, then, good for us, because we're needing good strong arms and backs around here. You look like a sailor, too."

"Able Seaman Jack Parker. And this is Boatswain O'Toole. We come all the way from Boston."

"Well, that's quite a trip, and I'm pleased to meet both of you. In fact, we can use all of you if you've a mind to join my gang."

Sergeant Bowen was of no mind to relinquish his authority, and when he seemed to hesitate, Gordy the shipwright knew exactly what to say.

"Now you'll be in overall command of your men, Sergeant. The way this will work is that I'll just give you your work detail every morning and you'll be responsible for getting' the job done in your own way. Agreed?"

"Couldn't ask for better than that," agreed Bowen, shaking Gordy's hand.

Kinkaid felt a bit left out, having his command join Gordy the shipwright's workgang without even a word of acquiescence from him, but now the shipwright came over to him and said, "You come up with these boys, Sir."

"Yes. I'm Lieutenant Kinkaid of the Continental Navy."

Well, I'm glad to meet you, Sir. I'm Gordon Wells, shipwright. I work for General Arnold and I hope you don't mind me corralling your men like that, but General Arnold has put me in charge of fitting out his completed ships and boats after they're built at Skenesboro and I need every man I can find."

"That's what we come up here for," said Kinkaid. "And I was told to give you all our seafaring equipage."

"And it'll all be put to good use, for anything I can't use

here I'll send on down to Skenesboro," said Gordy. "And Arnold will likely put you in command of one of these vessels, along with Captain Hawley that just showed up. Quite a story in that one."

"Yes, quite the seaman," gave Kinkaid, already tired of hearing about Captain Hawley.

"Rowed over five hundred miles in a week," said Gordy.

"So I understand."

"Are these men with you sailors?"

"Only two, but Sergeant Bowen there is a blacksmith."

"Well, we did need blacksmiths down in Skenesboro, but that was back in June. Now we have twenty-five of them and only four working forges, so I guess you can keep him."

Kinkaid felt more than a twinge of disappointment, not because blacksmiths weren't needed, but that Sergeant Bowen would remain with him, it seemed, instead of being sent down to Skenesboro where the blacksmiths worked. It's not that Kinkaid didn't like him, but more that his trust in the man had been sorely tarnished during the trip up, and besides, he didn't seem to get along with O'Toole very well and figured it wouldn't be long before the two of them would have it out once and for all; at least those were the reasons why Kinkaid looked forward to bidding farewell to the big sergeant.

Gordy turned now to admire the boat he had been working on and asked, "What do you think of her, Lieutenant?"

"Well, I can't say as I'm familiar with this type of vessel."

"Arnold calls 'em Spanish galleys. This is the second one that's come up from Skenesboro. The first one we called the *Congress*; she's at Crown Point. Three more are still under construction, and the last of Arnold's fleet. He stopped building gundalos and started on these because they can carry a lot of firepower. They'll be dangerous, is what

Arnold says, and that's what counts."

Kinkaid looked her over. She looked about sixty feet long, with a squared-off stern and with short, stubby masts with a lateen sail hanging at an angle from both masts. In addition to the monstrous 18-pounder at the bow, he could see another couple of heavy cannons protruding from her cabin, aft, probably 12-pounders. Poking through her gunports was a mix of 4-pounders and 9-pounders, six guns on each side. She was obviously meant for one thing and one thing only; to carry as much weight of cannon as could be squeezed aboard her. She would indeed be dangerous, but with that strange rig, could she sail?

But Kinkaid didn't have much time to think about the sailing qualities of the vessel, because when Gordy noticed the sailing ship coming up the waterway in the distance, he shouted, "Lordy, here comes Arnold! Let's get those cannonballs and powder aboard, men! And where the hell are those armorers?"

It was late in the afternoon by the time the sloop *Enterprise* drew alongside the dock, a ship once named the *George* that Arnold had taken from the British the summer before while aboard the *Liberty*, another ship that he had taken earlier.

And here came Arnold now across the gangplank as soon as it was laid down and secured, in a neat and tidy dark blue uniform with buff trousers.

At thirty-five, Arnold was dark and swarthy, handsome and stout, with a hawk-like nose, dark curly hair and a barrel chest, and he walked quickly, strode, really, although with a pronounced limp from the wound he had received at Quebec.

But that didn't take away the feeling of drive and energy that seemed to emanate from the man as he strode down the dock, shouting, "Gordy, I see some of your men standing behind those barrels over there, smoking. Put 'em to work or send 'em home! The British aren't going to wait until we're ready, you know!"

"Just a five minute break, I told 'em, General," returned Gordy. "And we've about finished arming the *Trumbull*, Sir."

An aide to General Arnold tagged along behind him and Arnold turned to him and said, "Major, go up and tell General Gates that I have returned from Skenesboro. Tell him that the ague is still laying our carpenters low but that progress is still being made. And tell him I still need more nails and spikes and oakum; and blocks and pulleys, too. And some shoes and clothing would be nice. Oh, and tell him that the *Washington* is almost finished, the *Lee* is coming along, and the keel of the *Gates* has been laid. And of course let me know if he has any instructions for me."

"Yes, Sir," said the major before he left in great haste to see General Gates in the fort, for it seemed that anybody and everybody around General Arnold acted in great haste.

Now Arnold turned his attention to the row galley that Gordy had been working on and he said, "I don't see any swivel guns along the bulwarks, Gordy. I want a dozen or more swivel guns on her, wherever you can find the space to rig 'em."

"I'm having the armorers fit those this afternoon, Sir,"

"Well, it's afternoon already. Where are they?"

"I believe they're still finishing up over on the *Boston*, Sir. But with those swivels and a few odds and ends we should finish her by tonight."

"Well, that's good, then, for I'll need her, and soon. And the last of them should be coming up in a day or two, from what I've just seen in Skenesboro."

A cooper was pounding on the metal hoop of a barrel just behind Arnold and the General turned and watched as the man struggled to unbend the warp he'd already pounded into the shape of the thing.

"Dear Lord, private, what are you doing to that poor barrel."

"Well, Sir…"

"Aren't you a trained cooper?"

"Well, I'm still learnin', Sir; started as a coffin maker."

Arnold strode over and took the hammer out of the man's hands and commenced to flip the barrel over. Then he started pounding on the opposite end, and while he was doing that he started spinning the barrel with his other hand and guiding it with his left foot. The barrel was all out of kilter, with one side bulging out while the other side looked caved in, but after a few revolutions and more vigorous pounding that barrel starting spinning perfectly formed.

"There, that's how it's done," said Arnold, stopping the barrel's spin and tossing the workman's hammer back to him.

Now Arnold spotted two soldiers walking down the pier. Each carried a long oar on his shoulder, but instead of taking them to one of the gundalos along the pier they started heading to the trail that went to Mount Independence, and so he called out to them.

"Say, you two with the oars!"

The two turned awkwardly and one almost bashed his friend in the face with the flat of his oar.

"Where do think you're going with those oars?"

"Well, Sir, uh, we thought they'd make good tent poles," stammered one.

"I'll be damned if those fine oars will be wasted for tent poles. If you need tent poles, go out into the woods and cut yourselves a couple. Now, take those oars over to that gundalo over there and give it to them."

"Yes, Sir," said both sheepishly.

Only now did Arnold's gray eyes fix on Kinkaid standing nearby and he asked, "Are you that privateer captain, Hawley?"

"No, Sir. I'm Lieutenant Jonathan Kinkaid, of the Continental Navy. I just came up with Colonel Lucas's 3rd Connecticut Volunteers."

"That's good to hear. Damned good men, those Connecticut boys," said Arnold, coming close and shaking Kinkaid's hand. "Good to have you with us, Lieutenant. Is that your horse over there?"

"Well, it's not exactly mine, Sir, but I signed for it."

"Then it's as good as yours. Good-looking mount, and strong, too. Does she behave?"

"Strong as an ox and gentle as a kitten," Kinkaid had to say.

"I knew it. Well, you're going to have to turn her over to the fort, because you won't be needing her any more. I've got a job for you, Lieutenant," said Arnold without fanfare. "Have Captain Dingle at the fort's stable sign your chit for you so you won't be responsible for her. Don't worry; she'll be well cared for. Have you ever captained a ship, Lieutenant?"

"Uh, no, Sir."

"Well, you will now. I'm making you the captain of that row galley over there. She's called the *Trumbull* and has enough firepower to make those lobsterbacks take notice. We started with three schooners and that sloop there, but they're fitted with little more than popguns, two and four pounders. And those gundalos over there will serve too, with a heavy gun or two aboard 'em, but they're awful light and get blown about in a stiff breeze, and with their open decks the crew has to get under tarps to get out of the weather. Why, they're really little more than oversized bateaux. I had hoped to build a 36-gun frigate but never had the men or the materials, but these row galleys are the next best thing!"

"I've never seen a ship rigged like that before, Sir."

"It's a lateen rig, Lieutenant. Like something an Algerian pirate might have, and it's as simple as it gets. Most of our men are lubbers, as us sailors like to call landsmen, and they won't get confused by the simple one line they have to pull on to hoist 'em. She'll maneuver better than any square-rigger, and when the wind is against her, she's equipped with oars. Why, she'll sail circles around those British ships, and pound them to hell while she's doing it. She's the first one complete, but I've got three, maybe four, more coming up from Skenesboro in a week or two. Now I know me making you a captain don't mean squat to the Navy, which means you'll still be a lieutenant in your service, so you'll be an acting captain, and I can't do anything about that, but you'll be a bona-fide captain to me and that's what counts. Are you following me, Lieutenant?"

"Yes, Sir."

"Good, let's go over and I'll show you what I mean. Did you bring a crew with you?"

"I regret to say that I only brought two sailors with me, Sir, and half a dozen carpenters recruited from a Connecticut militia regiment. And some supplies and tools, as well."

"Well, I was hoping we'd get some real ship's carpenters, not more house carpenters. I also sorely need more real sailors. You can't just take soldiers and put them on a ship and call them sailors and expect them to perform like sailors. But I suppose beggars can't be choosers, so we'll have to see how many sailors we can find amongst those 3rd

Connecticut men you came up with, to fill out your crew. They just sent us up some New Yorkers from the city but they looked to me like trash dredged out of some gutter. No, I wouldn't trust a single one of them to take a shit in the woods, so I sent the lot of them down to Waterbury who put them to work chopping down trees. Hell, half of 'em will probably end up chopping their own legs off. Do you know they gave each and every one of 'em a bounty, to come up here? Can you believe that? What a waste. Why, gutter trash like that is worse than useless to us."

Kinkaid had been sent to advise Arnold in the building of an inland fleet, but it seemed that he had been sent too late. No man to waste time, Arnold had already been advised as to what kind of a fleet to build or else he had employed ideas of his own, having spent a good deal of his youth aboard ships, plying his trade from New England to the Caribbean. Either way, the ships and boats had already been built. Even so, Kinkaid didn't feel the least disappointed, for Arnold had just made him a captain of his first completed row galley and was talking to him like an equal.

VII

First Command

Kinkaid had to run to catch up to Arnold as he strode over toward the dock where the *Trumbull* lay, explaining, "That damned fool of a Dutchman, Colonel Wynkoop, was put in Command of Lake Champlain by General Schuyler, and do you know the first thing he did was put a stop to building these galleys; can you believe it? In fact, instead of building ships he wasted half a forest of damned fine lumber and a regiment of good strong soldiers and carpenters to build that damned stupid stockade down at Skenesboro, as well as a bunch of fancy barracks, like a stockade and barracks was going to stop the English from coming down Lake Champlain. Well, I had to have that self-important jackass arrested when he fired on two of my vessels for sailing without his orders, like he owned Lake Champlain, and it was a blessing in disguise that he did that, because now he's being packed off to wherever he came from in the first place, and I've got General Waterbury down there, in charge of building more of these galleys."

Arnold was a whirlwind of dash and energy. He spoke fast, too, and had a lot to say, and Kinkaid simply listened and tried to keep up with all the information he was providing.

They stood in front of the vessel now and Arnold asked, "Well, what do you think of her?"

Kinkaid looked the craft over from stem to stern. Her lines were pleasing as she sat long and low in the water. Her sides were painted red, and with her rounded bow and squared off stern she looked solidly built, with heavy scantlings. She was heavily armed as well, with six gunports to a side, as well as having holes cut for six sweeps on each side. And Gordy was even now having the armorers fit swivel guns along her thwarts, deadly anti-personnel cannons to be used against men on an open deck of an opposing vessel. But because of her short raked masts and the way she was rigged Kinkaid felt unsure about her and only said, "She looks sturdy enough."

"I'll say she is; and dangerous, too, and that's the important thing. She's armed to the teeth and I doubt the British have anything like it. I heard Captain Hawley was coming up. I mean to put him in command of the *Royal Savage*. She's up at Crown Point. She's our biggest schooner and what they call my flagship, and I realize you'd probably prefer getting something like her, but I'll tell you, she's only lightly armed and won't do near as much damage as these galleys."

"Captain Hawley arrived with thirty sailors, along with myself and the 3rd Connecticut Volunteers, just this morning, Sir."

"Good, we'll need every man we can get. Now, did you report in to General Gates?"

"Yes, Sir. He was quite helpful and said we could set up our campsite wherever we wouldn't be in the way."

"You won't need a campsite. You'll live aboard, along with your crew. You'll need to train 'em and drill 'em and there's no time to waste, because we're not going to be hanging around here for long. The first galley is already up at Crown Point; the *Congress*. And the last of my galleys are about complete and they'll be coming up here over the next few weeks for their final fitting out. Then we'll be off up the lake to see what the British are up to and I'll expect you and your ship to be ready for them by then."

"I'll do my best, Sir."

"Now I'm going to pay a visit to all the vessels, make sure they're keeping up with our preparations and seeing to anything they might need. In the meantime you get your men aboard and squared away. I'll come back later and we'll go over to see the officer in charge of the 3rd Connecticut Volunteers about finding some men to fill out your crew. Let's see, you've got ten now, which means you'll need about fifty more."

Arnold no sooner left when Sergeant Bowen came up to Kinkaid and asked, "Where are we supposed to camp tonight, Sir?"

Boatswain O'Toole was with the sergeant and Kinkaid told the both of them, "We're all to move aboard that row galley over there, the same one that you and your men helped fit out today. She's called the *Trumbull*."

Both looked surprised, and Sergeant Bowen said, "You don't say, Sir?"

"You heard me, Sergeant. Go tell the men to bring the wagons up and get everything aboard that we'll need. Everything extra that we brought along for a ship's use we'll turn over to Gordy and his workmen."

"Who is to command us, Sir?" asked O'Toole.

"I am."

"Why, that's good to know, Sir," said O'Toole. "But have we enough men to crew her?"

"Don't worry; General Arnold will make sure we have enough men."

Kinkaid heard the men cheer when Sergeant Bowen told them the news, and they soon had both wagons drawn up beside the dock where the *Trumbull* lay and, their spirits high, they began hauling everything out of the back of both wagons and stacking it on the dock while Bowen and O'Toole decided what would come aboard and what would be turned over to Gordy and his work crews.

It was pretty exciting, seeing the men turn to with a purpose, not that they hadn't been busy all day helping to get the *Trumbull* fully armed, and the sun was low in the sky when Kinkaid noticed Arnold coming back.

With no other officers assigned to him, Kinkaid had some quick decisions to make, and so he said, "Sergeant Bowen, you're in charge when I'm away from the ship. I will better inform you as to the extent of your duties later. And Corporal Sanderson, you'll serve as my quartermaster and purser. You'll be in charge of keeping our daily log, all written records, our pay, and keeping track of our provisions and equipment."

"Yes, Sir."

"From now on that will be aye, aye, Sir."

"Aye, aye, Sir."

"Now, Sergeant, I need to go with General Arnold for a couple of hours, so I'm leaving it up to you to get everything properly stowed aboard. Have O'Toole and Parker help you."

"You can count on me, Lieutenant."

Kinkaid then went with General Arnold to see Colonel Lucas of the 3rd Connecticut Volunteers, camped at the base of Mount Independence, concerning the recruitment of some likely sailors and gunners to fill out his crew.

As always, Colonel Lucas was more than cordial and eager to help, congratulating Kinkaid on his new command and saying, "I'll have fifty or so of my best men with sailing experience report to you by early tomorrow, Lieutenant."

It had been an eventful day and it was dark by the time Kinkaid returned to the *Trumbull* where most of the tired men were already asleep, and what he found surprised him. Not only had Bowen installed a comfortable cot for him along the aft bulkhead of the cabin, but he had even put up a canvas screen so that he could have a bit of privacy, something that Bowen had not been asked or ordered to do, and it was much appreciated. It was also good to finally stretch out and relax and have a moment to contemplate all that had happened.

Kinkaid was greatly impressed by General Arnold, thinking him a highly intelligent, active and practical leader, with good ideas and high hopes to back them up. Even more than this, he was inspired by the confidence that Arnold had shown in him by making him a commander of one of his first new row galleys that he expected so much from, and a ship named after the governor of Connecticut, at that. But these thoughts also brought up doubts. Kinkaid had never commanded a ship before and knew little about leading men, or even how to sail the ship he had been given. The one thing he was sure of was that he had a lot to learn. But he also felt a great determination to do his best and live up to Arnold's expectations. But being very tired, all of these thoughts and worries were soon obliterated as he drifted into a deep and dreamless sleep.

It was the first night in over a week that Kinkaid hadn't slept on the hard ground and he awoke the next morning to the sound of waves gently lapping against the hull. Realizing that the sun was already well up and that he had overslept, he jumped up and grabbed his clothes, feeling guilty that he had overslept on his very first morning aboard, not the thing a responsible ship's captain would do.

He heard a shuffling of feet and there was Corporal Sanderson, poking his head through the curtain.

"Coffee, Sir?"

"Uh, thank you, Corporal, but I…"

"I've informed the men that you'll be up on deck after you've shaved and had your breakfast, Sir."

"Very good, Corporal."

Sanderson had saved him, it seemed, but he quickly washed his face in the basin and shaved so fast that he gave himself a good nick on his chin that kept dripping blood as he quickly put on his uniform.

He picked up his hat and was about to go up on deck when Sanderson arrived with a plate full of bread and cheese, and so he wolfed down a thick slice of bread with a large chunk of cheese on it, washing it all down with the bitter coffee, and almost choking on it in his haste.

He found Sergeant Bowen, Boatswain O'Toole, and Jack Parker on the deck when he came out of the cabin. The first thing he noticed was that the deck was severely scarred and dirty, no doubt due to all the workmen, and unavoidable during the fitting out process.

He also detected the aroma of bacon coming up out of the after hatch and he surmised that Watkins was down below, making breakfast for the crew, which also made him realize that the other men were still down below and probably asleep, but having overslept himself he could not very well make an issue of the matter, and so, after returning their greetings, he said, "I believe I'll simply have a look about the deck."

"Shall I accompany you, Sir?" asked Bowen.

"If you wish."

Unlike the smaller gundalos with their open decks, the galley *Trumbull* was built much like a schooner. She had a completely enclosed gun deck from stem to stern, with gunports cut through her bulwarks. She also had a proper forecastle as well as a quarterdeck above the stern cabin where partitions could be thrown up to house officers. The crew quartered on the gun deck, stringing their hammocks out of the weather and between the guns, with a five and a half foot overhead. In fact, the design of her hull was quite traditional; it was her sail plan that was unfamiliar to him.

Meant more to familiarize himself with the ship than a formal inspection, Kinkaid went up to have a look at the quarterdeck first, with Bowen tagging along behind.

Instead of a ship's wheel there was a tiller with an eight foot long handle, connected directly to the rudder, and instead of a binnacle there was simply a box in front of the tiller, holding a compass, a half-hour glass, and a small brass ship's bell. Along each side were racks that held their sweeps, long fourteen-foot oars that could be used to propel the ship for extra speed, in light airs or against the wind. At each corner of the quarterdeck were narrow, small-bore swivel guns mounted on the gunwale. And hanging limply from a stern jackstaff was a red and white striped flag with the words DONT TREAD ON ME across the face.

Upon turning around Kinkaid noticed that Boatswain O'Toole and Jack Parker had also followed the two of them up to the quarterdeck and now all three had to awkwardly jostle aside and say, "Excuse me, Sir," as he went back down the four-step ladder to the main deck.

Moving forward, Kinkaid noticed the neat coils of medium-sized rope along the deck, as well as the racks for holding belaying pins and others for cannonballs for more swivel guns. He then looked up at the short mainmast, just abaft the center of the ship and in front of the cabin hatch, rising about fifty feet over his head, with a very long double-spared yard cantered at a forty-five degree angle about halfway up, with a neatly furled mainsail attached, and he took in the arrangement of halyards for the raising and lowering of the yard. Ratlines ran up above where the yard was attached on either side of the vessel and just abaft the ratlines were the main shrouds that supported the mast.

Forward was another hatch leading down to the gundeck and crew's quarters. And just before the slightly raised forecastle rose the foremast, an exact replica of the mainmast except that it was stepped just ten feet behind the stubby bowsprit, and with the same arrangement of halyards, ratlines and shrouds. A single fluked anchor hung lashed to the beam of a cathead on the port side of the bow, and in the center of the forecastle was a small but sturdily built capstan.

"Sturdy scantlings throughout," observed Kinkaid, feeling like he had to say something to Sergeant Bowen, but also realizing that only the stoutest beams would suffice to keep the heavy cannons from shaking the ship to pieces. "And the sail plan and rigging seem about as simple as it gets."

"Yes, Sir," said Bowen.

"Except for all the scars and dirt on the deck, she's rather shipshape and Bristol-fashion," added Kinkaid. And then realizing that Sergeant Bowen probably had little idea as to what he was talking about, he said, "I take it that all of our tools, supplies and equipment, our muskets and powder, and all personal effects were stowed in their proper places?"

"Yes, they were, Captain; everything in its proper place," said Bowen, and then realizing that O'Toole and Parker were standing right behind him Bowen felt compelled to say, "These two were more than helpful in showing us where things were supposed to go, Sir." But instead of leaving it at that, Bowen had to add, as if making up for giving the two sailors some credit, "Except they insisted that we bring those four barrels of water aboard, and I can't understand that. Here we are on a lake with millions of gallons of good fresh water and they want to bring water barrels aboard."

"Well, what if we run aground in some mucky bay?" said O'Toole. "Then you'll be thankful we brought some good clean water aboard."

Kinkaid ignored the bickering but his grimace of displeasure had the effect of silencing the two. He wanted to go below and check on the gundeck, except that he knew he would be disturbing the others, and so he said, "Well, then a good job in securing everything last night, men. And I really must thank you, Sergeant, for the effort you made to…uh, ensure my sleeping comfort."

"Well, we can't have our captain bein' elbowed by riffraff, now can we, Sir," said Bowen, jabbing O'Toole in the ribs, whereupon O'Toole and Parker both graciously laughed at the joke.

"Speaking of sleeping," began Kinkaid uncertainly enough, "I realize I overslept a bit myself this morning, but hereafter I shall expect the deck hands to turn out to scrub the planks and polish the brass and fittings every morning before breakfast. And breakfast shall begin at seven and go no later than seven-thirty."

"Yes, Sir," said Bowen.

"I'll see to it, Captain," said O'Toole.

"I'll have a roster of duties and watches made up once we have a full crew, as well as a daily schedule."

"Very good, Sir."

Kinkaid then returned to his cabin to give the other men a chance to wake up and have their breakfast, and they no sooner filled their bellies with bacon and beans when the roll of a drum got everyone's attention.

When Kinkaid returned to the deck he saw a column of men on the road that came down from Mount Independence, marching toward the dock, fifty-six men in all, men selected by Colonel Lucas from his 3rd Connecticut Volunteers, and so Kinkaid went out to greet them.

Their drummer boy looked no older than fifteen but he could certainly make a racket with that drum of his and when the column halted at the pier their man in charge had to say, "That's enough, O'Donnell," before he would quit banging on it.

"Corporal Bell, reporting as ordered with your shipboard detail, Sir," said the short, freckled soldier with a stiff salute.

"Are these men all sailors?" asked Kinkaid, finding it hard to believe.

"Well, most claim to have had some sailing experience, Sir," he said dubiously.

"Good to have you and your men join us, Corporal," said Kinkaid, returning the salute. "No need to be formal. Come aboard and we'll get you all squared away."

And so it was that Kinkaid was provided a full complement of sixty-six men in all, and he wasted no time in dividing up duties and assigning the watch bill with Corporal Bell's assistance in telling him which men among the Connecticut Volunteers had the most sailing experience and which would serve better as gunners, and Corporal Sanderson soon had a roster of the ship's crew, dividing them up into port and starboard watches. There was also a simplified daily schedule for the crew to follow as well as a list of rules of shipboard behavior.

It was only that evening, after posting the roster and schedule and rules of the deck on the door of the cabin that Kinkaid learned what he was up against as a new captain. He was about to go up on deck when he heard some of the men talking on the other side of the door and something made him stop and listen for a moment.

"Take a look at this," he heard one voice say. "It tells us when we gotta get up, when we're supposed to eat, when to expect drills; even when to go to bed. And look at this stuff about disobedience and punishment. Hell, a man isn't even allowed to spit on the deck."

"Didn't you hear? A captain's word is absolute," said another.

"And that's another thing; this captain of ours seems awful young. Any of you ever hear of this Kinkaid fellow? I heard he wasn't even a real captain, but just a lieutenant."

"But a lieutenant in the navy is equal to a captain in the army," someone else pointed out.

"Well, it seems like they coulda given us someone with more experience, and less rules. Why, a man's got more freedom in a monastery."

"Since when were you ever in a monastery, Riley?"

"Well, the only reason I joined this scow was because I heard the navy gave you liberty."

"Liberty? That only means you get to leave the ship once in a while."

"Like when?"

"Well, for special occasions."

"Like when your mother dies."

"My mother already passed, bless her soul."

"Well, then you're out of luck, Riley."

"That's right, Riley," came the familiar voice of Corporal Bell, "And since when did you expect the navy to be any different than the army?"

"At least you're getting' a bonus."

"But I'll need to leave the ship to spend it," said Riley.

"Which means you'll be a rich man when this war is over," said Bell. "Now, you men get to work or I'll find a job for you."

It was only the next day that Arnold came by, and after giving the men a short pep talk, telling them how the country was counting on them, and that the important thing was in delaying the British as long as they could, he took Kinkaid aside.

"I want you to take her out now," Arnold told him. "Just get the feel of her today, of how she handles, and sort your crews out. Now, I know they all come to you claiming shipboard experience, but I wouldn't put too much stock in that, seeing as they've been promised extra wages to serve on the lake. Just take it slow and easy at first as they get adjusted. And I wouldn't bother with any gunnery practice just yet; maybe in a couple of days. And before you do, first make certain that you instruct your entire crew, and especially your gunners and loaders, as to the proper safety precautions in the handling of powder and slowmatch. We don't want any foolish accidents. Later we'll go out in groups and conduct some exercises that'll help us fight together as a fleet."

It was good, practical advice, coming from a man who had started out as a sea captain himself, and as soon as Arnold left, Kinkaid turned to the men who were all looking expectantly at him and he said, "Are you men ready to set sail?"

A chorus of eager exclamations resounded off the cliff behind them.

"Make ready to cast off!"

O'Toole was forward and Jack Parker was aft and they showed the men how to single up and then cast off their lines that set the ship adrift, and then showed them how to neatly coil the lines on the deck so that they would be out of the way and not be tripped over.

Even so, there were plenty of men tripping over one another, simply because every man was overly eager to do his share and lend a hand and Kinkaid could tell right away that it was going to take some time before they would work as an efficient team, for it was obvious that less than half of them had ever sailed a ship before.

But somehow the ship drifted free of the dock without incident and the foresail was raised after a lot of shouting and questioning what O'Toole was shouting about, because to some of them it seemed like he was speaking a foreign language, using phrases like, "Cast those gaskets off the fores'l!" and "Heave to on that peak halyard!" and "Belay on that throat halyard!" and so on, but with Jack Parker's help in adjusting the angle of the sails the ship backed into the current of the inlet while Kinkaid steered her out into the middle of the channel where she caught a northeast breeze and off they went.

It was exhilarating to be on a ship again, seeing the triangular sails billowing out and hearing the gurgling of water along her cutwater, and when Kinkaid looked about the deck he could see that all of the men were feeling the thrill of embarking upon a great adventure.

The whole day was spent out on the water, practicing all manner of exercises; hauling and reefing sails, switching to the oars, tacking and wearing ship, coming about and running with the wind, and although there was a lot of confusion and misinterpretation of orders at first, there was already a real feeling of camaraderie and accomplishment by the time they returned to the dock as the sun was setting, as evidenced by the way the men were talking excitedly among themselves.

And as far as Kinkaid was concerned, the *Trumbull* turned out to be everything that Gordy and General Arnold had said she was; a sturdy, very maneuverable and easily handled row galley gunboat, and with her heavy armament would be sure to make the British fleet consider her a serious opponent.

They went out very early again the next day, and every day after that, except that Kinkaid allowed the crew to sleep in on Sundays, when they could wash and mend their clothes, air their bedding and attend to personal concerns after attending a service consisting of O'Toole reading a few passages from the Bible and then discussing them, and it was amazing how quickly the men learned how to sail and adjusted to shipboard routine. Even the man called Riley seemed to have forgotten his gripping about the ship's rules and its captain after becoming proficient in the workings and handling of the lateen sails.

In fact, they became adept enough at putting their galley through her paces that it was only a few days later that Kinkaid set about organizing their gun crews, first instructing them in the proper safety precautions of handling powder and slowmatch and then holding dry fire drills before allowing them to load and then fire each gun once, and it was both nerve wracking and thrilling to hear their noise, especially that of the massive 18-pounder at their bow that caused the entire ship to lurch under their feet when it was discharged.

They worked long and hard at learning all there was to learn about the sailing and fighting of the *Trumbull* in that first week, and more than once after they'd returned to the dock all hot and sweaty from their exertions Sergeant Bowen would say something like, "Lordy, I wish I had a beer."

And somebody else would say, "Don't we all."

And then Bowen would say something like, "I want a beer so bad I can smell it."

And once Private Metcalf said, "You know, I thought I smelled beer once too, Sarg, while I was at my oar. A good strong whiff I had too. It was the strangest thing."

But Bowen just said, "Shut up, Metcalf, you're making me drool."

Boatswain O'Toole proved to be a godsend the way he took charge of the gun deck and the ship's boats and other equipment and soon formed a deck crew who were out every morning before breakfast scrubbing the deck and polishing the brightwork, and already those scars left by the workmen and armorers had been scrubbed away and the decks gleamed a pale blond like fine furniture. O'Toole also put his knowledge of herbs to good use, tending to the various injuries and illnesses that a few of the men sustained.

Able Seaman Parker was also a valuable addition, not only for the way he carried out every order with alacrity and efficiency, but simply by the way he carried himself he set an example of what a squared-away sailor should be. He also had a friendly and patient manner about him as he demonstrated to the others how to be real sailors without making them feel less than. He also proved to be a helluva gunner and Kinkaid made him the gun captain of the two 12-pounders in the after cabin.

It turned out that Corporal Bell had once been a topman on a whaler out of Nantucket and so Kinkaid placed him in charge of the sail handlers, those men tasked with hauling up the sheets and actually sailing the vessel. He was smart and had a sure way about him that his men respected.

And while Kinkaid would have admitted that Sergeant Bowen would not have been his first choice as first mate, Bowen proved a hard worker and a good man to have aboard, always ready and willing to lend a hand here and there, and to fix anything that needed fixing. In addition to being in charge of the marine guard that enforced Kinkaid's orders aboard the ship, he also held regular drills with his soldiers, having them turn out for inspection, practicing with boarding parties, holding firing drills with the swivel guns, climbing and taking station in the ratlines, and having regular target practice, both on the shore and aboard ship.

Not only that, but all of Bowen's men started referring to themselves as marines, giving them a distinction as a special unit. Even more than all this, those days of purpose and frantic activity proved once and for all that keeping busy was Sergeant Bowen's salvation, whether Bowen realized it or not.

It wasn't long before Private Metcalf proved to them all that he was by far their best shot, winning every shooting contest, and some of the men were even beginning to call him "Sureshot." It provided the once slovenly soldier a good deal of pride to learn that he was better at something than most men, to the point where he seemed to become more shipshape and military every day.

It only took about a week out on the open water before the ship and her crew began to function as a ship should, to Kinkaid's immense relief and satisfaction, for the men were not only learning the essentials of sailing, but they were even beginning to look and talk like sailors, wearing scarves around their necks and jackknives on their belts, and picking up the lingo from O'Toole and Parker and Bell and a few others who had sailed aboard ships before, and it was amusing how the men soon began to replace the word floor with deck, wall with bulkhead, ceiling with overhead, and "Yes, Sir!" with "Aye, aye, Captain!"

They sailed every day for weeks, mostly under fair and sunny skies, but even through thunderstorms, and more often of late a cold, hard rain, but still Kinkaid drilled them and kept them out on the water and they sometimes returned soaked and shivering. Once they were caught in a hailstorm, and it hailed so hard that it left the men stunned and bruised as they toiled at the sweeps.

But by now they could do anything with their galley, turn her like a dime, switch from sails to sweeps and make way against a full gale blowing into their faces, and then switch back to sails in the blink of an eye. Not only that, but they excelled at gunnery, loading and firing and reloading in record time, able to blow any target out of the water as if it was something they were born to do.

So proud was he of them, these men who had worked so long and so hard, earning the right to be called "crew," that he had them all gathered in the waist one Saturday morning before they went out and he said to them, "Men, I have to say that I had my doubts after that first day on the water when everybody was tripping over each other and nobody knew their larboard from their starboard side, but now I can't tell you how impressed I am by every single one of you. Why, I'd match this crew against any crew in the whole Continental Navy."

The men cheered at the short speech, and no one cheered louder than Private Riley, for in fact they were really cheering for themselves, and then Sergeant Bowen said, "Too bad we don't have anything to help us celebrate, Captain!"

But now O'Toole stood up where he'd been sitting beside

the tiller, smugly smoking his fancy pipe, since he knew only too well that the accomplishments of the crew had been facilitated in great measure by his expertise and patient instruction, and he said, "Seaman Parker, I think it's time we tried some of that good sweet water we brought with us all the way from Boston."

And the way he said it, kind of sly-like, told even the thick-headed Sergeant Bowen that there might be more to those water barrels than met the eye.

Now Jack Parker asked, "May I have your cup, Sergeant?"

Bowen untied his tin cup from his belt and handed it to Parker, who held it under the spigot of one of the barrels of "water," and what came out to everyone's amazement was a golden liquid that left a thick head of foam at the top.

He handed the filled cup back to the Sergeant and Bowen partook heartily, draining his cup and leaving a mustache of foam on his upper lip.

"I'll be damned if that ain't the best Boston water I ever tasted!" he exclaimed to a roar of approval from the deck.

"I knew I smelled beer," said Private Metcalf as he handed his cup to Parker. "I just knew I smelled beer. Once you smell beer, you don't forget the smell of it."

Kinkaid watched tolerantly while all the men, including the young drummer boy, had their cups filled and Sergeant Bowen's refilled, but then he said, "Two cups per man should be enough to celebrate, seeing as it's still early and we've a day of sailing ahead of us. But we'll finish that barrel tonight and have a real celebration, seeing as how tomorrow is the Sabbath."

"And I might even dance for you," said O'Toole, raising his cup and doing a little jig on the quarterdeck to the amusement of all.

Later, as they were heading out into the inlet, Kinkaid

overheard Sergeant Bowen asking O'Toole, "Now, why did you let on that those barrels were filled with water all that time, Boats?"

"Because if I'd a told you they held beer, you woulda drank it all up before we even got up here."

"That's right," agreed Parker, "and then what would we have celebrated with?"

Sergeant Bowen just shook his head in exasperation, knowing the two sailors were right, but realizing that they were probably the only ship in Arnold's fleet with their own supply of beer and that their evening meals would henceforth be washed down with a few cups of the frothy brew took away some of his exasperation.

That night their first barrel of beer was finished off as Kinkaid had promised them, celebrating their transformation into sailors.

One man brought out a fiddle and another produced an accordion and they sang a few songs and Private Riley and Boatswain O'Toole even danced a jig on the open deck before they finally grew tired enough to fall asleep in the wee hours of the morning, like the proud and self-satisfied sailors they had become.

But there remained a few who stayed awake for most of the night, reminiscing about their service thus far, and Kinkaid was able to learn something of their exploits and even more about the general they served under.

VIII

A Night Breeze

One of the men who remained awake out on the deck that night was Corporal Bell, and most of the others were from his group of Connecticut Volunteers, men whose names Kinkaid barely knew as yet and so they were little more than shadows and voices to him at the time as he lay on his cot, feeling the cool night breeze coming through his stern window as he listened to the men on the roof of the cabin.

At first they talked of their homes and families and of places they'd been and some adventures they had.

But then one man with a rough voice asked, "Corporal Bell, I heard you served under Arnold last summer."

"That I did," said Bell, "and even before that I come up with him when they took Ticonderoga."

"You don't say? Now, I heard that was Allen's Green Mountain Boys that did that."

"Well, the men were Allen's, and I was one of them at the time. Arnold had recruited some of his own men in Massachusetts but they hadn't arrived yet. But that's about all I can say for Allen and his so-called boys; a bigger bunch of sniveling, ill-disciplined drunks and hicks you ever saw. They're named right, I'll say that."

"I heard they were a rough bunch," said a high-pitched voice.

"Not by my book, they weren't, and I'm ashamed to call myself one of them now. Why, they couldn't follow an order. And if they felt ornery enough they wouldn't even follow Allen's orders, but threaten to go home if he didn't coddle 'em."

"How the hell did they ever take the fort, then?"

"Well, it was Arnold's doing. He come up from Massachusetts with the only bona-fide commission, although they wouldn't listen to him. But Allen was only a colonel because he called himself a colonel and he had to agree to share the command with Arnold."

"So it was Arnold led them against the fort?"

"Well, sort of. I remember it well, that night we come up to the door of the fort. There was only that one sentry there and he half asleep…and when he noticed us he tried to shoot off a warning shot but his powder had gone damp and he couldn't even do that."

That brought a few chuckles from the men.

"Yep, all he could do was skedaddle through the door…and that's when Arnold had the presence of mind to follow right behind him, and of course Allen wasn't about to be left behind and so we all scuttled through that door and there we were, right inside the fort, and not a soldier to be seen."

"So what did you do?" asked the high-pitched voice.

"Well, we ran all over the place, looking for soldiers to shoot, but they'd barricaded themselves into their barracks while Arnold and Allen were trying to locate the commanding officer, a man named Delaplace. I remember, we were all standing at the bottom of the stairs of the officer's quarters and there was this British officer at the top of the stairs who demanded to know who we were and what we were about. Well, Allen was all puffed up and he starts shaking his fist and says they'd better surrender their fort or he'd turn his men loose and kill ever man, woman and child in the place. They had their families with them, some of them. But Arnold had a cooler head and promised them they'd not be harmed but be treated like gentlemen, and the commander steps out in his nightshirt and after a few words from Arnold we all went over to the barracks and their soldiers all came out meek as lambs and stacked their arms. Only about forty-five men and officers in all, not counting their women and children, and only half of them fit to fight. Easy as pie."

"So Arnold took charge, then?"

"Well, for that moment, at least. After that Allen's men went crazy. They broke into the fort's rum room and rioted, pillaged and plundered the place. Hell, they stole or destroyed about everything they could get their hands on. Well, Arnold and Allen had some choice words then, I can tell you that."

"What did he do; Arnold, that is?"

"Well, what could he do? Both Arnold and Allen sent couriers out saying that the fort had been taken, but they refused to obey a single order of Arnold's, preferring instead to run riot over the place when some firm discipline was called for. Why, they insulted him to his face and two of them even shot at him. And then this man named Mott came up and held a council of war with some of his cronies and they gave the command to Allen."

"So that left Arnold out in the cold."

"So to speak," said Bell. "Allen didn't know the first thing about military service and his men didn't care about much other than their next drink, but they refused to serve under Arnold and even threatened to go home if he so much as looked at 'em sideways. Even so, he managed to get some of us to work for him, building up the fort's defenses. That's when I cast my lot with Arnold. At that time the fort had been run down quite a bit. Some of the walls had tumbled down and there were even cannons that had fallen into the lake, and Arnold did everything he could to retrieve those guns and build the walls back up, in spite of Allen and his 'boys.' Hell, Allen didn't have the first inkling of what to do, much less understand that the key to controlling Ticonderoga as well as Crown Point meant control over the lake. Well, luckily some of Arnold's men began to show up and most of the Green Mountain Boys began to disappear when the rum ran out."

"I heard that's when Arnold resigned."

"Well, he had to because nobody was in charge of appointing a proper commander up here," said Bell. "Good thing Washington put Schuyler in charge and it was Providence alone that had Schuyler meet Arnold in Albany as one was coming and the other was going. That's when Schuyler recognized a smart fightin' man when he saw one and made Arnold the commander up here. And he didn't waste any time, either, but got the sawmills and ironworks going."

"Wasn't that about the time Arnold's wife died?"

"That's right," said Bell. "She was only thirty years old. But his father died only three days later and he heard about both their passing while in Albany. Not only did he have to bear that news, but then the Massachusetts Congress told him they were refusing to pay his expenses. They denied all his claims for all the money he had shelled out to keep his troops in clothing, ammunition, food and supplies, not to mention for oxen and horses and cows. Why, you can't imagine all that Arnold had to pay for out of his own pocket. Hell, they even had the gall to tell him he would have to get a receipt for every single item from that damned fool Colonel Easton, who hated Arnold with a passion for no other reason than because Arnold knew what a cowardly fool he was."

"Now that weren't right."

"No it wasn't," said Bell. "But do you know that Arnold, like the good soldier he is, came right back up here and took charge anyway? Not only that but he went right out and took the schooner *Liberty* and properly armed her. Then they went up to St. Johns with her and took the sloop *Betsy*, too, right out from under the noses of the British. They renamed her the *Enterprise*. Hell, that made Arnold king of the lake."

"I heard Allen showed up again with some his boys," said someone.

"He did, that weasel," said Bell with a laugh, "and with about ninety of his men. They were a sorry lot, too, as usual. They had come up in some leaky bateaux, and of course they didn't think to bring any supplies with them so they were starving, as well. But you know what, Arnold shared all our food with them anyway, in spite of the way they had treated him. Then that fool Allen wanted to go up and take St. John's...can you believe it? After Arnold already took it. But I knew Allen only came up with that idea in order to outdo what Arnold already did. Arnold tried to talk sense into him. Hell, the British had been aroused by now and were sending reinforcements from all over Canada to St. Johns after his raid, and besides, there was no reason to bother with St. Johns since we already had their best ships and control over the whole lake at that point."

"I take it Allen didn't listen too well to what Arnold had to say," guessed the man with the rough voice.

"How'd you guess," answered Bell. "Allen and his fools went paddling up the lake, but they no sooner came skedaddling back with their tails between their legs and their asses full of buckshot when the British surprised them the next morning. They even left three of their own behind."

"I haven't heard about Allen lately."

"Yeah, whatever became of him?"

"Well, it's funny you should ask," said Bell, "because after a while even the Green Mountain Boys had become fed up with Allen's bragging and lying and foolish ideas that usually resulted in some of them getting killed or getting a load of lead in their ass and they pretty much deserted him. So the damned fool went up to Canada and thought he'd recruit a bunch of Canadians to help him take Montreal. Well, his Canadians skedaddled at the first sight of a British redcoat and left Allen standing there by himself. Yup, got himself captured and shipped off to England, last I heard."

"Now ain't that a hell of a note?" said the rough voice.

"But what about the charges that were brought against Arnold?" one man wanted to know.

"That was all started by that damned lying fool, John Brown, one of Allen's minions."

"You mean the one that claims Arnold is a liar and a thief?"

"One and the same. He left the fort as soon as it was taken and reported to the Continental Congress that the fort had been taken, and if you'd a heard what he told 'em it sounded like he took the place all by himself."

"He's still causing no end of trouble for Arnold, is what I hear," said someone.

"Well, there's more than a few of them. Not only Allen and Brown, but there's James Easton, too, who took the news of Ticonderoga to Boston and the Massachusetts Congress where he claimed it was he who took the fort singlehanded. Even the British commander of the fort, Captain Delaplace, ended up refuting that."

"It seems Arnold is a fighter, not a politician," said a voice.

"Well, that's the long and the short of it," said Bell. "And that wasn't the worst of it because then Massachusetts and Connecticut and New York all started arguing about who was responsible for taking the fort, and not only that but nobody wanted to claim responsibility for it; they were all afraid that King George would get mad and send soldiers to attack their state. Not only couldn't they decide who was to command the forts up here but they wanted to remove all the cannons from Ticonderoga and send them down to Fort George, giving up the fort and Lake Champlain as well as all those farmers and pioneers up this way."

"What a bunch of sniveling cowards," said the rough voiced man a bit too loudly, waking a number of men from their drunken slumber. "It's a wonder they ever agreed to fight this war," he added more quietly.

"Well, you can say that again," said Bell. "Even though the Massachusetts Congress gave Arnold his commission and sent him up to take and then command Ticonderoga, he was from Connecticut and didn't know any bigwigs in Massachusetts. Nor did he know enough bigwigs in Connecticut willing to stand by him, so nobody ever said a word in his favor. But do you know that while all the politicians in Massachusetts and Connecticut and New York were worried about restoring harmony with England, that's when Arnold started thinking about invading Canada? He knew they weren't ready for war, either, and had few enough men in arms to defend their own country, much less threaten ours."

"Did you go up with him?" asked a man.

"No, I left here when Arnold did. Went back home and joined up with the 3rd Connecticut."

"I heard it was hell up there," said the rough voice.

"Well, I was there, with Dearborn," said a new voice, a voice so calm and quiet that Kinkaid had to strain to hear him. "Over two hundred of us died just on the march up there. It was worse than hell, men dropping left and right from starvation, disease and the cold. Some of 'em just got lost. Lordy, was it cold. Hell, it was October when we crossed that God-forsaken Maine wilderness, and a lot of us ended up barefoot because we'd been reduced to eatin' our shoes. I was never so hungry in my life. We ended up eatin' all our dogs."

"Ah, jeez, that's rough," said someone.

"What's dog taste like?" asked the high pitched voice.

"Well, even the eyeball of a dog is better than shoe leather or a cartridge case if you're hungry. But that weren't the worst of it. All our boats fell apart and we had to carry everything we had. And we were wet all the time. Even when the bogs froze over we'd break through and end up walking with frozen trousers. It's like walkin' with boards tied to your legs."

"Gives me a shiver just thinkin' about it," said Metcalf.

"Well, I'd just as soon forget that part myself. But then Montgomery was killed when we attacked Quebec. It was New Year's Day, during a snowstorm. Arnold took a bullet in his leg, and almost lost it. But I gotta hand it to him; he brought all of us survivors back with him, in spite of Sullivan's foolishness and most everybody starving or coming down with smallpox. Arnold's proved himself in my

119

book."

"I agree," said another. "Why, he'd the best damned General we ever had or ever will have."

"Except nobody appreciates him."

"We do."

"But the shame of it is that small men can say things about a man of character and get away with it."

"Small-minded people always hate big-minded people."

"That's right, and it's always the ignorant fools who are listened to and more ignorant fools who believe what they say."

"That's cause most people are ignorant fools."

"That's why I hate 'em."

"Hate who?"

"People."

"Well, people will believe the most ignorant and outlandish statements you can imagine."

"And even some you can't imagine!"

Now that calm and quiet voice spoke again, and he said, "The entire history of humanity is a battle of truth overcoming ignorance."

It sounded so profound, but then perhaps it was only the way it was said; whatever it was, the statement seemed to hang in the air for a moment.

But of course they couldn't let their carping be brought to an end by too much profundity, and so the rough voice said, "Jealousy and ignorance are the curse of humanity."

"And those same damned jealous fools are still spreading lies about Arnold."

"Did you hear what just happened with the Hazen court martial? Hazen was acquitted of all charges. Can you believe that?"

"Sure I can. It was because Hazen's buddies were all on

the court and they all hated Arnold."

"I heard they all went out to dinner afterwards."

"That's when they decided to have Arnold arrested because he complained about the verdict," said the high-pitched voice.

"Yes, but Gates had enough of their shenanigans and had the sense to dissolved the court," the rough voice reminded them.

"But where is the justice?"

"Ignorant fools!"

"People! I hate 'em!"

The men had really gotten themselves worked up by now, but when a few voices of protest asked them to "hold the noise down!" they became quiet again.

In fact, nobody said a word for a while. And then the rough voice said, "Which only goes to show that the fightin' man on the scene hasn't got a chance against the man who has the ear of a cowardly politician who can sit home beside his fire and let another, braver and better man do his fightin' for him."

"Hear, hear!"

Another voice said, "Thank God saner heads prevailed and they formed the Continental Army or we'd all be bowing to King George today."

"Amen to that," came a general chorus of agreement before the men settled down, and eventually they all grew quiet and went to sleep.

The next morning, being Sunday, Kinkaid let his men sleep in and tend to their personal chores. He also made a point of getting to know the names of those men whose voices he had listened to the night before.

The rough voice turned out to be a rather short and dour man named David Goodman. He had once farmed near

Danbury, but when his wife and child both died of cholera he decided to leave the place and join the army. All of thirty, Goodman was older than most of Kinkaid's volunteers, but had worked on a fishing boat before acquiring the farm and knew his way around a boat. And because of his sure manner and gruff voice the men looked up to him and voted him captain of the 18-pounder.

The man with the high voice was a tall and fair young man with a wispy mustache named Solomon Dyer, only seventeen years old and a favorite among the crew. He was one of those who may have stretched the truth a bit when they asked for experienced seamen, but nobody would fault him for wanting to serve, and he was a smart boy and learned fast. He said he came from the city of Hartford, where his father owned and operated a book store. He was also a bit high strung and reacted strongly when the cannons were fired, which drew some laughter from some of the others, and Kinkaid suspected that Dyer meant to prove his courage by begging Goodman to let him serve as a loader on the 18-pounder, something Dyer was now inordinately proud of, even though his knees still trembled every time the gun was discharged.

But Goodman was glad to have Dyer be one of his loaders if for no other reason than the young man reminded him of his own son who had died at the age of thirteen, and the two were often seen together about the boat.

The third man, the one with the quiet voice who'd gone with Arnold up to Quebec, was named Joshua Timmerman. He was about twenty-five and sported a long but wispy goatee that blew in every direction. He seemed to be a thoughtful and modest young man and nobody seemed to know much about him for he didn't talk much, especially about himself, but some of the men began referring to him as "The Wise," for his sage observations on people and the world at large.

Kinkaid also had a chance to reflect on what he had learned about Arnold from the men's conversation of the night before, and his admiration of the man who he served under, the man who had sight unseen made him captain of the *Trumbull*, only increased. He also learned how Arnold's men felt about their commanding general and somehow it made them even bigger and better and more loyal than he already knew them to be.

By now two more of the row galleys came up from Skenesboro, the *Lee* and the *Washington*, and they were being fitted out with their own formidable set of heavy guns, and crews sought for them.

After allowing the various ships and boats to go out on their own for a week to organize and sort out their crews and learn the foibles of their ships, Arnold gave each captain of his fleet one of his signal books, and then he took them all out and had them sailing in various formations. Then he divided his ships and boats into two attacking forces and they practiced mock fights against each other, and afterwards the results were discussed, with successes complimented and mistakes rectified.

All this practice and maneuvering and mock fighting made them start to feel like they were a force to be reckoned with, and there was much brave talk of meeting the British fleet.

It was around this time that Kinkaid found himself seriously considering what they might be facing. And so, when Arnold visited the *Trumbull* one day Kinkaid asked him what he thought the British might have for a fleet. Well, the way Arnold changed the subject and started talking about how the lateen sails could be adjusted this way or that in various situations, Kinkaid could only conclude that

Arnold either didn't know or was reluctant to tell him.

But a few days later some prisoners were brought in, a couple of British officers who had been waylaid by the brave work of some American infiltrators under a man named Whitcomb who had become famous for shooting and killing a British general on an earlier foray up above St. John's where the British fleet was rumored to be. And it was through those prisoners that, smug in the knowledge that the American rabble had no chance against the might of the British Empire, some information about Carleton's force came to light.

They learned that the British had at least three sea-going ships that had been taken to pieces and reconstructed at St. John's, only a hundred miles north of Fort Ticonderoga; the ship *Inflexible*, 18; the schooner *Maria*, 14; and the schooner *Carleton*, 12. It seemed they also had a big gunboat that they referred to as a radeau, and called it *Thunderer*, and that it was armed with 12 heavy guns and two howitzers. And there was also a gundalo named the *Loyal Convert*, 7; in addition to twenty smaller gundalos converted into gunboats, each mounting a large caliber cannon, and an indeterminate number of armed longboats, the whole force manned by almost a thousand men.

It was a formidable fleet and gave much food for thought, but some of the men couldn't believe that the British were smart enough or ingenious enough or had enough gumption to have taken ships apart and put them back together again, and were convinced that the prisoners were exaggerating.

As for Arnold, he encouraged such thinking because he didn't want his men to become discouraged, but he also redoubled his efforts to go around to all of his ships and boats and tell the men how good they were and how the British were going to be taught some lessons by them, that they would underestimate the Americans and their sailing and gunnery skills, and that their overconfidence would prove their downfall.

He also told them that their earlier show of force, when he had taken his schooners and sloops and gundalos up to St. John's earlier in the summer, had had the effect of delaying the British fleet for at least another month; that the sight of them had made the British doubt that they were ready to meet them, and all of this talk brought a rousing cheer from the men and helped buoy up their spirits.

Kinkaid knew that even if the British had delayed because of Arnold's show of force they would not have just frittered that time away, but would have used that month's delay to build even more ships to oppose them. But he also realized that Arnold had a point about delaying the British, knew that it didn't matter what their fate would be when they finally met their fleet; that the important thing was keeping them from coming down the lake before the fighting season was over.

IX

The Shadow of Death

It was almost October now. The leaves were in their peak and the hills were ablaze in vibrant color. The weather was already turning brisk and cold, and there was a feeling of snow in the air.

Arnold knew that the British would not dare to move their army in winter conditions. If he could only delay them for another month, then the British would be forced to wait until next spring to advance, giving the colonies the time they needed to better prepare their forces. All knew that they would have to come soon or not come at all.

It was these thoughts and more that occupied Kinkaid's mind as he prepared his ship and crew after General Arnold ordered the entire fleet to set sail for the north end of the lake, and the last thing they brought aboard was one of the large Indian war canoes that Arnold insisted all of the row galleys carry. And of course the not-so-bright Private Metcalf had to joke about them being useful as life boats in case they were sunk, which only brought a chorus of hisses and boos from the others, having a view of such thoughts being abominable if not treasonous, to Private Metcalf's chagrin.

The part of Lake Champlain that Kinkaid had seen and sailed upon thus far was nothing compared to the vast expanse of water beyond Crown Point that Kinkaid now found himself upon as the cliffs on the New York side and the forests of the Vermont side receded into the distance and the shores of the lake opened out as the fleet headed north against a cold, stiff breeze.

Their first destination had been to sail six miles up the inlet to the fort at Crown Point where the lake narrowed down to almost nothing.

Crown Point had also started as a French fort and marked the southernmost incursion of French influence in the northeast. Built in 1731 it had been named Fort Frederic during the French and Indian War. But that is where the similarity to Fort Ticonderoga ended, for as a fort Crown Point wasn't very impressive. It had nothing like the thick stone walls of Ticonderoga, nor did it sit impressively at the top of a mountain. Instead, Crown Point sat right there at the end of the peninsula, right on the flats at the edge of the water. But her cannons could at least reach any ship that tried to sail down the narrow inlet and that was what made the spot a place worth holding.

But the fleet didn't tarry long at Crown Point; just long enough to pick up the schooner *Royal Savage*, under the command of David Hawley, the famous privateer captain, who now led the way with Arnold aboard.

Close behind in a three ship screen was the schooner *Revenge*, Captain Seamon, the schooner *Liberty*, Captain Premier, and the sloop *Enterprise*, Captain Smith.

Behind them were two of their heavily-armed row galleys, the *Congress*, and Kinkaid's *Trumbull*. The galleys *Lee* and the *Washington* were still being fitted out at Ticonderoga and the *Gates* was yet incomplete down in Skenesboro, having been delayed by the ague.

Spread around the central fleet of these gunboats were the gundalos, *New Haven*, *New York*, *Connecticut*, *Providence*, *Philadelphia*, *Boston*, and *Spitfire*.

In all they were thirteen ships, carrying fifty guns and manned by about four hundred men, and it was a glorious sight to see them all formed up as a complete fleet for the first time, flying their red and white striped flags with the motto "Don't Tread on Me" snapping in the breeze.

"Why, it almost seems like a miracle, Captain," said O'Toole at the tiller, his wild hair tied back in a ponytail that blew in the wind.

It was true, for what Arnold had accomplished in a few short months did seem miraculous, especially with little or no help from Congress, with scarce and shoddy tools, even scarcer carpenters and skilled builders, and with a lack of the most essential and simplest materials like nails, spikes, oakum, canvas, and iron fittings, not to mention a lack of shoes and clothing for the workers, soldiers and sailors.

But there it was, a grand fleet, and it gave them a thrill to be a part of it as Arnold took them up through The Narrows at Split Rock where the lake widened to six or seven miles, with the misty blue Adirondack Mountains to the west and the snow-topped Green Mountains of the Hampshire Grants (later Vermont) on the eastern side.

They all knew that a meeting with the British fleet was only a matter of time, but this didn't seem to concern Arnold as he took them even farther north, putting them through their paces with all manner of fleet exercises, and at sunup of the next day Arnold called for a gunnery exercise, calling for two shots from the heaviest cannon aboard each vessel, a prize to be awarded to the first gun crew that could fire twice, and now all the gun crews on every ship were standing by their loaded weapons, ready for Arnold's signal to begin the contest.

Aboard the *Trumbull* this meant the 18-pounder at the bow, captained by David Goodman and with Solomon Dyer as a loader.

"I'll bet we win," said Dyer with a broad grin, but you could tell he was nervous by the way he fiddled with his sponge swab.

"That's right, Sol, we just have to be faster than anybody else," said Goodman, giving the boy a wink, and then blowing on the slowmatch cupped in his hand.

"We're already faster than anybody else," answered Dyer.

"And here's your chance to prove it."

"I wonder what the prize is?"

"Probably a barrel of rum."

"A barrel? I don't know if that'll be enough," joked Sol. "I got a mighty powerful thirst."

"Hell, Sol, you get drunk on a pint of beer," Goodman reminded him. "But don't worry; we'll help you with that barrel. Now shut up and get ready."

Kinkaid watched as the signal flag rose up the flagstaff aboard the *Royal Savage*.

"Ready! Fire!"

Goodman touched off the gun and it roared out and jerked back on its truck as the dirty white smoke blew out over the water off the starboard side.

"Reload!" yelled Goodman.

Dyer ran in front of the gun and frantically rammed his wet sponge down the tube before quickly drawing it back out. Then he grabbed a fresh charge of powder from the powder monkey and began to ram it down the tube. That's when the gun went off, blowing him over the side.

"Man overboard!" shouted Goodman, shocked to have

seen Dyer go flying out over the bow like that.

"Heave to!" shouted an equally shocked Kinkaid and the sails were quickly dropped.

Everyone was looking out over the waves as the ship drifted to a stop and finally Parker shouted and pointed, "Just aft, off the starboard quarter, Captain!"

They could all see the body now, barely floating on the surface, the waves washing over it, and it was plain to all that Dyer was dead.

But it was sickening to watch as his body was grappled and hauled aboard, with the arms and legs dangling like they weren't really attached to anything. In fact, his left arm was missing at the elbow, and the body just flopped on the deck like a blood-soaked rag doll, his face a horrible mess, with one eye bulging out of its socket.

"It's like every bone in his body is broke, Sir," observed O'Toole.

"Dear God, it doesn't even look like Sol," mumbled Goodman.

Arnold had noticed that the *Trumbull* had broken formation and so he brought his ship up behind them to ascertain the problem as the men respectfully covered Dyer's broken body with a square of canvas.

"A loader was killed when our gun discharged prematurely!" shouted Kinkaid across the gulf.

Arnold grimaced and shouted back, "Take yourselves into that bay over there and give him a proper burial! I'll expect you to rejoin the fleet by noon!"

"Aye, Sir."

It was still eight in the morning as they headed for the shelter of the bay, and Kinkaid found himself considering what had to be done as he stood on the quarterdeck, and how it was to be done. After all, it wasn't as if there was a manual or even a set of written instructions that he could consult. He had never officiated a military funeral before, and he wanted to do it right.

The first thing he did was to ask O'Toole, "Say, Boats, I wonder if you might recommend something appropriate from out of your Bible…something that I might read at the service."

"Why, certainly, Captain; I believe I know just the passage."

Sergeant Bowen had been standing amidships and overheard the exchange and now he came over and suggested, "We'll need an honor guard, Captain, and I'd like to lead it, if you don't mind, Sir."

"Of course, Sergeant."

"And a flag over the body would be a nice touch, Sir. And of course we'll have O'Donnell on his drum."

"That sounds perfect," said Kinkaid appreciatively.

By now Goodman noticed the others conversing and he came over and said, "I'd like do whatever I can, Captain."

"Uh, well…"

"You can be one of the pallbearers," said Bowen.

"And you can help me stitch Sol up in that canvas that's over him," suggested O'Toole.

"I'd like that very much," said Goodman, and off the two went to prepare the body.

In the meantime Sergeant Bowen went about rounding up six men to fill out his honor guard, as well as the rest of the pallbearers. And of course young Patrick O'Donnell would beat his drum.

It wasn't exactly a warm day, for the wind was brisk and cold, but at least the sun was trying to break through a scattering of clouds, and it wasn't long before the ship was anchored and the funeral party headed to shore in the ship's

131

whaleboat, everybody bundled up in their heaviest coats and with scarves around their necks.

Leaving only a bare minimum crew aboard, they then waited until the boat had made three trips in all to get everyone ashore, the body coming with the last load, lying on a wide plank with one of their flags draped over it.

In the meantime the honor guard and the pallbearers, with Sergeant Bowen leading them, went up with a pick and some shovels onto a small rise about twenty yards from the beach. Kinkaid thought it was the perfect spot for a grave, but he waited for Goodman to say something.

Goodman stood there, looking out over the lake for a minute or so before he said, "I think this is the place." And that is where they dug the grave, next to a couple of wind-blown cedars.

Then they went down and lifted the body out of the boat, shouldered by Goodman and the other five pallbearers as little O'Donnell beat out a somber dirge on his drum. The honor guard led the way with their muskets on their shoulders, followed by the body and then the others, with Kinkaid bringing up the rear.

Goodman almost tripped and fell as he stumbled over a rock at the shingle where the beach ended and the land began.

"Easy, there!" came O'Toole's warning, but thank goodness the body didn't fall and they continued up to the top of the rise where everyone eventually gathered, about forty men in all, and they managed to lower the body into the grave with only a minimum of clumsiness.

O'Donnell stopped his drumming now and O'Toole brought his Bible out of a satchel that was slung over his shoulder and he handed it to Kinkaid standing at the head of the grave.

A stiff wind came up at that moment and Kinkaid had to clutch at his hat to keep it from blowing away, and then O'Toole helped him open the Bible to the appropriate verse.

O'Toole had chosen the Twenty-third Psalm, and after pulling his hat down hard around his ears, Kinkaid read aloud:

"The Lord is my Shepherd; I shall not want.

He maketh me to lie down in green pastures.

He leadeth me beside the still waters.

He restoreth my soul.

He leadeth me in the paths of righteousness for His name's sake.

Yea, though I walk thought the valley of the shadow of death,

I will fear no evil; for thou art with me.

Thy rod and thy staff, they comfort me.

Thou preparest a table before me in the presence of my enemies.

Thou annointest my head with oil; my cup runneth over.

Surely goodness and mercy shall follow me all the days of my life,

And I will dwell in the House of the Lord forever."

Everyone murmured, "Amen," at the end.

And then Sergeant Bowen said, "Attention!" and the honor guard stood in a rigid line.

"Prepare for volley fire!"

The men brought their muskets up to their shoulders, cocked their pieces, and then aimed out over the lake.

"Fire!"

The muskets spoke almost as one and after a few moments of silence the men began to drift away back toward the beach while Goodman stood there and watched the pallbearers filling in the grave.

Once back aboard the ship, Kinkaid felt unsure about the ceremony, felt that perhaps he could have done something more for poor Solomon Dyer, although he could not for the life of him imagine what that might be. But he felt guilty somehow, felt that he had only managed to muddle through the event, and so he allowed the crew to finish off their second barrel of beer as they headed back to the fleet so as to help them drown their sorrow and they were all pretty subdued by the time they regained their place in the formation around noon.

Not that they didn't appreciate the beer, but so shocked was everybody over the loss of young Sol that nobody even inquired as to which ship won the gunnery contest, or even what the prize had been, but Sergeant Bowen and the crew of the *Trumbull* would be even more careful now with the rationing of their last two barrels of beer.

That evening, after a day of shifting winds and intermittent showers, the fleet anchored in The Narrows about seven miles north of Split Rock, along the western shoreline, and that is when Kinkaid held a serious meeting before the crew had their dinner, lecturing them on the importance of making certain that sponges were thoroughly soaked before being rammed down a barrel as well as being careful to ensure that one's sponge was plunged all the way in to extinguish every remnant of a smoldering spark.

Solomon Dyer had been their first casualty, and though it was also a terrible tragedy, they all knew that it had been Dyer's own fault. Everyone had liked young Sol but he was too nervous for his own good, and David Goodman was the first to admit it after a couple of pints.

"Damn, I never should have let him join our gun crew," Goodman could be heard to say amidships after a desultory dinner. "Sol was always scared of that gun. He was too nervous and too quick." And everyone knew it was true, that in his haste he hadn't properly sponged out the barrel.

"It was almost like he was a sacrifice," said O'Toole.

"What do you mean by that?" asked Goodman.

"Well, first we have this miracle of a fleet and then Dyer is taken. Don't you see? It's like he was meant to balance things, so to speak."

"Well, I wouldn't know anything about that," said Goodman rather testily. "All I know is that poor Sol was too young to die, and I just can't see any right in it."

And then Metcalf, as if backing Goodman against O'Toole, said, "And I didn't see how the sermon had anything to do with dyin'."

"Well, I thought it was fitting," said O'Toole defensively.

Kinkaid too, heard the remark and felt stung by it, seeing as it was he who had read the sermon.

But then Goodman came to their defense and said, "I thought it was very fitting, since it had a lot to do with going into danger and overcoming fear."

All of which left Metcalf thoroughly confused.

Now the quiet voice of Joshua Timmerman spoke up and he said, "Especially since a funeral is more for the living than for those who have passed."

"That's right, Metcalf," said Parker. "Those words were for *you* to hear."

Everybody took a moment to think about Timmerman's words, and even Metcalf seemed to get the gist of it, for he sat there with his mouth open and nodding his head like he'd just had the revelation of his life and then he tried to recall some of the words of the sermon that was meant for him.

"Well, I'll need a new loader for my 18-pounder," said Goodman, breaking the silence. "Would you take the position, Josh?"

Timmerman looked up from where he sat and said, "I'd be honored."

It seemed the perfect choice since Timmerman seemed to have what Solomon Dyer had lacked; a quiet confidence and a calm and careful manner, qualities that operating a dangerous gun required, not that young Sol wouldn't be sorely missed.

Boatswain O'Toole could be seen reading out of the Bible more often after that, and overall the incident served to remind the entire crew that they were engaged in serious business and that they were at war, but some of them saw it as an omen of what was to come.

X

A Lesson in Leadership

Arnold had the fleet anchored along the western shore that evening, about seven miles up from The Narrows, and it was not long after the crews had their supper that a stiff wind started to blow, bringing a cold, stinging rain with it.

At first the wind and the rain was intermittent, mostly out of the north, with short periods of calm in between, but by the time the sun had set the wind had grown violent and constant and the driving rain came down in buckets.

The gundalo *Spitfire* was closest to shore and Kinkaid could see the men aboard her trying to stay dry under a tarp they had rigged over the bow and midships, but he felt sorry for them, having no roof over their gun deck and little in the way of a dry cabin to retreat to.

All of the ships and boats were straining at their anchor cables and so Kinkaid hardly slept that night for fear that their anchor wouldn't hold. His fear increased about three that morning when the wind shifted from the north to the northeast, threatening to blow the fleet onto the shore.

It was at first light when O'Toole shouted, "Boat approaching!"

They could all see through the rain that it was Arnold in a

whaleboat from the *Royal Savage*, coming out to inform all his captains that they would leave the anchorage at two that afternoon and that he would fire a gun to signal their departure.

Of course they all hoped that the wind would mitigate by then and they would all safely get away from the dangerous lee shore. But instead of mitigating the wind grew even stronger as the noon hour drew near, bringing forceful gusts that pushed their ship sideways and sent cold waves sloshing over the bow.

Realizing that the fleet wouldn't be able to tolerate much more of such pounding before one of them broke their anchor hold and foundered on the beach, Arnold had the signal gun fired at one that afternoon instead of waiting until two.

"Make ready to get under weigh!" shouted Kinkaid which brought the men scrambling up onto the wet and blowing deck.

It took all of twenty men hauling on the anchor cable before they were able to pull the iron cross aboard and then it was a close thing, getting a reefed fores'l up as they drifted free, because the wind and the waves were pushing them toward the shore.

"Let out one more reef!" shouted Kinkaid, realizing they needed more driving power to buck the waves, and hoping it wouldn't blow the sail out.

Only when he was sure that they were actually heading out into the lake did Kinkaid look up through the driving rain and take note of the *Spitfire* off to starboard.

She had also raised her anchor, but being a flat-bottomed gundalo the wind and waves were having their way with her as she tried to claw out to open water, and instead she was being pushed dangerously toward the beach, unable to overcome the momentum of the waves.

"Boat to larboard!" yelled Jack Parker.

At first Kinkaid feared that they were about to collide with another ship but when he looked off the port beam he was surprised to see only a small rowboat with a single man aboard, the dark figure rowing like a madman over the turbulent waves.

"It's Arnold!" bellowed Sergeant Bowen.

"I don't believe it!" shouted O'Toole.

Sure enough, it was their commander in the tiny boat.

"Either he's the bravest of the brave or he's a reckless lunatic!" exclaimed Metcalf.

It was hard to believe that Arnold had come out in that maelstrom, and alone at that, and as he drew nearer they could see that the boat was being tossed about like a cork, with Arnold swaying this way and that as the boat bounded over one wave and then was almost lost from sight as it dipped into the trough. But Arnold grimly rowed on, his feet planted wide apart to keep his balance and gripping the oars for dear life.

Arnold skirted around their stern and then went heading toward the stricken *Spitfire* whose captain had by now sensibly tossed his anchor back over the side to save his ship from foundering in the shallows.

Kinkaid continued to watch as Arnold drew alongside the *Spitfire*, and then after conferring with Captain Ulmer for a few minutes he started rowing back toward the *Royal Savage*, almost five hundred yards out in the lake, and it was even more difficult going against the wind and the waves as his boat was tossed this way and that, and there were times when it seemed that he was actually being blown back.

In the meantime Ulmer had thrown out both his anchors, furled his sail and was simply trying to ride out the storm under bare poles.

But the whole fleet must have had their eyes on Arnold as he bounded over the waves in his tiny boat, and it was almost an hour later since they first spotted him before he could be seen drawing alongside the *Royal Savage*.

"He must be exhausted," said Parker, sighing with relief.

"Or else he's the strongest man in the fleet," observed Bowen, a strong man himself.

The wind was howling in the rigging of the *Trumbull* as Kinkaid took her out into the middle of the lake behind the other vessels as the rain came down in buckets, soaking the men on deck and cutting down visibility so that the *Spitfire* was soon lost from sight and nobody would have betted that she would long survive before being driven ashore and broken up.

The sloop *Enterprise* led the fleet and it was a wild ride as they went running with the wind and the waves, south down the lake, back past The Narrows and Split Rock.

The gundalo *Connecticut* was just off the port beam of the *Trumbull* when they all heard a loud crack like the sound of lightning, and when they looked in her direction they could see that her mast was toppling over, and an instant later her bow was smothered under a heap of canvas and cordage, her crew scrambling to hack it all free.

"Gone by the board!' exclaimed O'Toole.

She was barely steerable now and was drifting sideways with the wind and the waves buffeting her.

Kinkaid was thinking they would have to jury rig some kind of a sail, however temporary, if they hoped to gain some ability to maneuver, when the schooner *Revenge* came up to her and took the stricken gundalo under tow.

The fleet was about to reach the shelter of Buttonmould Bay along the eastern shore when the *Enterprise*, who had been leading them down the lake, went aground when she made her turn into the bay too soon.

But she was only stuck in the mud and in no real danger; in fact she served as a marker buoy for all the other ships in the fleet to stay clear of the shallows there as they rounded the headland and made for the shelter of the bay, and by late that afternoon she floated free again and joined the others.

They remained there for the rest of that day and that night, for the wind kept howling and the rains kept falling, and it was a good thing because the men were exhausted and needed a respite. Of course those aboard the *Connecticut* didn't get much rest because they had to put up a new mast and that was no small feat.

The next day still brought no reprieve from the storm and so the ships remained in the shelter of the bay. Many wondered what had become of the unfortunate *Spitire*, and there were rumors that she had foundered and so everyone could only hope that most if not all of her crew had made the safety of the shore and had not perished.

It was beginning to grow dark when O'Toole noticed the ghostly shape emerging through the veil of another rain shower.

"Why, it's the *Spitfire*!"

She had lost the bateau that she always dragged behind her, but otherwise looked none the worse for wear, and she soon made for the middle of the fleet and everyone cheered when she dropped her anchor.

The storm raged for another two days, keeping the fleet trapped in the bay, for they would never have been able to tack back up through The Narrows in the face of that wind.

It was after their fourth day stuck in the bay that Kinkaid decided to finish writing that letter to Solomon Dyer's parents, informing him of their son's unfortunate demise and telling them that he had been a brave and resourceful young man, was well liked by his mates and that he would be greatly missed by the service in general as well as all those aboard who had served with him.

He had just read the letter over for the last time and signed it when a boat drew alongside the *Trumbull* with a message for Kinkaid from Arnold, asking him to meet him on the shore around noon.

The wind had mitigated somewhat by then and the sun peeked out now and again from the scudding clouds and it wasn't a bad day at all when Kinkaid took their whaleboat ashore and found a number of boats on the beach and all of Arnold's captains ashore.

He also found a roast pig sizzling over a big pile of hot coals just up the beach, along with a couple of makeshift tables that had baskets of bread and cheese on them, and bottles of wine and jugs of apple cider, too. There was even a fancy punchbowl, filled with a potent elixir of juice laced with rum.

"Good to see again, Kinkaid," said Arnold, coming down to meet him on the beach when he arrived and handing him a glass of punch.

"And you, General."

"As long as we can't go anywhere, I thought we'd put the time to good use by having a picnic. Come on up and join us; help yourself to whatever suits your taste and we're about to have a shooting contest. I should have told everyone to bring their favorite piece with them, but there should be enough muskets to go around."

Like everything else he did, Arnold had gone all out to provide a sumptuous feast for his officers, and even thought about ways to entertain them and help them get to know one another better in a relaxed atmosphere.

And so Kinkaid took part in the friendly competition to see who could best shoot an inaccurate and unfamiliar musket, a dubious distinction at best, and calling for more luck than skill, and it was good fun for all.

After the target practice, won by Captain Ulmer of the *Spitfire*, they all drank a toast to Congress and then another to victory, and then Arnold said they'd better put an end to the toasts or they'd never make it back to their ships and the men took the advice with a laugh but also for the sober reminder that it was.

Then they all went back down to the beach where someone had fashioned a horse-shoe pit and partners were selected to make teams.

Kinkaid found himself teamed with Captain Joshua Grant, of the gundalo *Connecticut*, the same one that had been dismasted during the storm.

Captain Mansfield of the *New Haven* then suggested they play for a penny a game, "Just to make it interesting," and it turned out that Kinkaid and Grant made quite a team, for they soon had a nice pile of pennies on one of the tables, bringing from Captain Hawley of the *Royal Savage* that he, "couldn't play against them any more or they'll take all my hard-earned pay," and it was a good joke appreciated by all.

It was a chance for Kinkaid to get to know his colleagues and what he found was a clear-headed and steady group. Not only that, but they were all quite cordial to him as the junior officer among them.

At one point Kinkaid went to partake of some of the food. He had just finished a good-sized portion of the succulent roast pig and was enjoying a glass of a very excellent Chardonnay while watching some of the others toss horse-shoes when Arnold came over to his table and sat across from him.

"I was sorry to hear that you lost a man during our last gunnery exercise, Lieutenant," he began. "Who was he?"

"A fine young man by the name of Solomon Dyer," said Kinkaid. "He was only seventeen."

"That's too bad," said Arnold. "I have a son who is seventeen. Make sure you write a letter to his kin."

"I just did, Sir."

"Good. And not an easy thing to do. Give it to me the first chance you get and I'll see it's sent out the next time I send a ship back to Ticonderoga for provisions and supplies."

"I appreciate that, Sir."

"How did it happen, if you don't mind my asking?"

Kinkaid explained how Solomon had been a nervous boy and in his haste had improperly sponged out the gun before placing the next charge.

"Hmm. A foolish mistake, then. He probably shouldn't have been made a gunner."

"No, Sir," said Kinkaid, feeling a twinge of guilt.

"Ah, but that's all water under the bridge now, and don't blame yourself, Kinkaid. We are all of us only human and cannot foresee every eventuality or purpose, and certainly have little power to prevent every tragedy. It's unfortunate, but accidents will happen. Did you hold a proper funeral for the boy?"

"We did, but I'm not sure if we did it right, Sir," admitted Kinkaid.

"Well, how did you do it?"

"We had an honor guard, and pall bearers, and most of the crew were turned out. We sewed the body in canvas and covered it with a flag. Then I read a passage from the Bible, and then my sergeant had his honor guard fire their weapons over the grave." He didn't mention the barrel of beer that he let the men finish afterwards.

"I don't see how you could have done any more than that," said Arnold. "In fact, that seems very thorough to me."

"Well, thank you, Sir."

They sat together in silence for a moment before Arnold said, "No matter our rank or station in life, or what privileges we may enjoy, every man is equal in the eyes of God, and so it is important that we recognize the supreme sacrifice of even the most foolish soldier or sailor under our command, for they deserve the highest honor we can give them and, well, if your true sentiments are any indication I am certain that you fulfilled that obligation with the greatest respect and conducted yourself in the highest manner befitting the occasion."

"I hope I did the right thing by him and his fellows, Sir."

Arnold patted Kinkaid on the knee and said, "If an officer is already held in esteem by his men, then it takes only the simplest word or gesture, so I would say you fulfilled your duty in an exemplary fashion."

"Thank you, Sir."

Arnold's officers' picnic turned out to be a most excellent feast and a very welcome change in routine, thought Kinkaid as he returned to the ship that evening, feeling quite relaxed and at ease.

It also occurred to him that Arnold must have had some inkling as to Kinkaid's uncertainty about himself. He couldn't imagine how this might be so, but to have engaged him the way he did seemed evidence enough. And it made him hold the man in even more esteem than ever, for he realized that Arnold cared not only for the men under his command by the way he took that tiny boat out on the lake during the storm in order to help save the *Spitfire*, but he also cared for those who commanded them.

More than this, it was a simple lesson in leadership that

Kinkaid would always remember and treasure, finding Arnold's words a valuable guide in certain and various situations throughout his career.

XI

The Most Expendable Officer

The storm finally passed and the wind once again blew from out of the south, and so the fleet was alerted to make ready to sail at eight o'clock that morning. But as they were about to leave the bay two more ships were seen heading toward them from the south and so Arnold once again fired his signal gun ahead of schedule so that the fleet would make sail immediately in case the sails turned out to be that of the enemy.

As it turned out, the two ships were identified as the newest of their row galley's, the *Lee*, and another gundalo, the *New Jersey*, and so happy was Arnold to see them that he had the entire fleet give them a salute as they met them in the mouth of Buttonmould Bay, with each ship or boat firing a single cannon, the salute returned by the *Lee* and the *New Jersey*, and the noise of the guns and the sight of all that white smoke drifting over the lake induced a lot of cheering and thrills up the spine.

Little did Arnold know at the time that the salute had been heard all the way down to Crown Point and of course everybody down there thought that the two fleets had met in battle, which had Gates calling an alarm for his troops to be ready to repulse an imminent attack and he even sent some reinforcements up to Crown Point. He also sent an armed bateau out with Lieutenant John Brooks aboard to find the fleet and ascertain what had happened.

The *Lee* took her place in formation right between the *Congress* and the *Trumbull* and Kinkaid could not help but notice how differently rigged she was in comparison with the other row galley's, for instead of twin lateen sails on two masts, she had a single square-rigged sail plan with a course and a topsail, along with a boom-and-gaff driver and two headsails attached to the bowsprit, commonly called a cutter by the British.

But now they were a proud fleet of fifteen ships as they headed back up through The Narrows and past Split Rock before a fresh breeze. The sun was shining and the sky was clear but for a few cirrus horsetails way up high, and it felt almost like a day with the regatta and hard to believe that they might run into a British fleet at any moment. Even so, the fleet seemed a glorious thing, and so powerful that many of the sailors were using words like "invincible" and "unbeatable."

Once, when they were all strung out in a line abreast formation across the lake O'Toole had exclaimed that they were "a line of battle," and they all felt a surge of pride to be a part of it, even Kinkaid, though in the back of his mind he knew that any officer in the British navy would have laughed at them comparing their puny ships with Britain's ships-of-the-line, massive sea-going vessels that carried anywhere from 64 to 140 heavy caliber guns on two to four decks. Why, not even a single one of their ships could have stood up to the might and power of even the smallest British frigate of 32 guns.

But that didn't take away the feeling of pride and power

they felt as they sailed up the widest part of the lake that day and the next, finally anchoring in the lee of Valcour Island, the halfway point between Ticonderoga and St. John's.

The next day they set sail to the north once again after Arnold had passed the word that their primary objective henceforth would be "to actively seek the enemy," and that their destination would be all the way up to Windmill Point where the Richelieu River began and even farther up the River, into Canadian territory to the Isle aux Tetes, only twenty-six miles from St. John's.

But they didn't have to go all the way to the Isle aux Tetes to find the British, for on the very next day, after arriving around two in the afternoon off the Peninsula of Cumberland Head, they spotted a group of about twenty men, some of them Indians, on the western shore.

Arnold's picket boats that day, the gundalos *Boston* and *Philadelphia*, were the first to see them, and when they closed near to the beach they fired their swivel guns at the enemy but with little noticeable effect except to send them scurrying into the forest.

Arnold quickly sent two whaleboats of riflemen out after them, and when Kinkaid watched the boats unloading at the beach he noticed that there were half a dozen Indians among the riflemen. He took a look through his telescope and studied the men in their buckskins and homespun, each carrying one of those long rifles. And then he noticed one Indian in particular, a familiar sight with his three feathers, red leggings and bright buckskin jacket. But what clinched it was seeing that big brown dog with him.

Kinkaid handed O'Toole the telescope and asked, "Do you see who I see?"

O'Toole took one quick look and said, "That's Captain Cloud, all right. And there's Little Scout with him. Looks like he works for Arnold after all."

Sergeant Bowen heard the exchange but said not a word.

The riflemen with their Indian scouts returned to the beach later that afternoon and it was soon ascertained that they had not made contact, but it was the first sign that the British were out in force and that they had their Indian allies with them.

With still no British fleet in sight, Arnold kept them sailing north, passing the large Isle la Motte and past Point au Fer and then right up the Richelieu to the Isle aux Tetes, and the men grew ever more nervous as they kept a close eye ahead of them, knowing they were in Canada now, and that St. John's was just up the river where the British fleet surely lay in wait, probably raising sail and about to come down the lake at that very moment, at least in everyone's imagination.

Arnold had the fleet stretched across the inlet that evening, so close together that not even a bateau could have scurried through, and this is how all the rumors were able to pass from one ship to the next as quickly as a leaf falls from a tree to the forest floor.

Arnold had also taken the precaution of sending some groups of soldiers and riflemen to camp upon the shore on either side, so as to ensure they wouldn't be ambushed from the banks while they slept. Even so, it was nerve-wracking, sitting there in the middle of the Richelieu River, right in Canada itself and so close to the British.

The *Trumbull* was the third ship in the line, stretching from the island, and anchored only a hundred yards off shore that evening. The men were finishing their supper of salt pork and beans, and O'Toole was seated next to the tiller, smoking his pipe.

Metcalf was whittling on a stick and kept looking nervously at the dark forest, and finally O'Toole said,

"Worried about Indians, Metcalf?"

"Who ain't?" replied Metcalf defensively.

"Well, I wouldn't worry too much. Arnold has those riflemen out to make sure they don't sneak up on us."

"But what if the riflemen get snuck up on first?"

"I suppose that's something to consider," admitted O'Toole, "but even then it don't pay to worry, because you won't hear 'em anyway."

"That's right," said Parker. "They're mighty sneaky in those moccasins they wear."

Now Private Riley got in on the conversation, affirming, "Why, you'll never even know when they've come and gone."

"That's right," said O'Toole, "You'll just never wake up."

"Or you'll wake up in hell and find your throat's been cut," mentioned Goodman with a chuckle.

"So I'd worry if I was you, Metcalf," said Bell.

Metcalf wasted no time in doing just that.

"Hell, they could sneak up on those riflemen, cut their throats, and then swim out to get us," said Metcalf, and he noticeably shivered at the thought of hundreds of painted savages with knives in their teeth slithering out of the black lake and over their gunwales in the black of the night.

"What do plan on doin', Metcalf," asked Bell, "live forever?"

"Well, I'd like to live as long as my grandpappy."

"How old was he when he passed?" asked O'Toole.

"One hundred and one."

"Damn," exclaimed Riley. "Now what do you suppose his secret was…to live that long?"

Metcalf never hesitated, but answered, "Grandpa said he lived that long because he stayed away from women and soap."

"Well, if he stayed away from soap, then I don't imagine he'd be troubled too much by women," said Timmerman, 'The Wise'.

"Except your grandpappy musta had a wife," said Bell.

"Oh, grandma didn't like soap either," answered Metcalf.

The men had a good chuckle over that before Goodman said, "Well, I don't know too much about the dangers of soap, but I do know that women can be dangerous, and I know enough to stay well clear of Indians."

"At least we're out here on the lake," observed Riley, "where we can see 'em comin.'"

"That's right," said Parker, "and the biggest boat the Indians have is a war canoe."

"Speaking of boats, I heard that Arnold is itching to meet the enemy fleet," said Goodman.

"I heard that, too," said Timmerman. "And you can't blame him for that; to show them what we've accomplished, to give him a taste of our gunboats."

"And I say let 'em come, too," said Jack Parker, talking the brave talk.

"What if they don't come?" said Metcalf, and everybody took that to mean that Metcalf hoped they wouldn't.

"Then we will have accomplished what Arnold hopes to do," said Timmerman soberly, "and that is delay the British advance for this year."

"But if they do come, do you think we're ready for them?" asked Metcalf.

"Why sure we are," said O'Toole. "Just look around you. Do you think the British have anything like what we built?"

"I wouldn't underestimate the British," said Timmerman, the voice of reason.

"Well, I doubt they could have done what we did," said Parker, "because if they had they'd be out here on the lake by now, and all we've seen of 'em so far is a few men along the shore."

"Have you noticed how Arnold has been sending one ship or another to reconnoiter every little bay, inlet and estuary from Crown Point to here?" said Timmerman.

"He has been doing that, now that you mention it," said Private Riley.

"So what do make of that?" asked Sergeant Bowen.

"I'd say he's probably making a chart of the lake," said Parker.

"Or there could be other reasons," said Timmerman kind of mysterious-like.

"Well, like what?" Metcalf wanted to know.

"I think he's formulating some kind of a plan."

"To do what?" asked Metcalf, swatting at a horde of gnats that had gathered in front of his face.

"Well, to defeat the enemy fleet, what else?" said Riley too loudly, like he was exasperated with Metcalf's stupid questions.

Timmerman didn't say anything after that, but just drew on his pipe like he knew what Arnold was thinking, and the others thought about what Timmerman had said and kind of took comfort in knowing that Arnold had a good plan up his sleeve and that he would somehow take the British by surprise.

Yes, it was kind of comforting...until O'Toole said, "Say, do you boys know the name of that island over there?"

"Why, that's the Isle of Tits," said Metcalf smugly, being the first to answer like he did.

"You mean the Isle aux Tetes," O'Toole corrected him. "It's French for Island of the Heads."

"So?" said Metcalf, annoyed over being corrected, especially over some stupid French name.

153

"Well, do you know why it's called the Island of the Heads?"

"Tell us," said Sergeant Bowen with a sigh, knowing that O'Toole would tell them anyway.

"Well, it just so happens that a big war party of Abenakis, probably over a hundred of 'em, ran into twenty-six Mohawks on that island a few years back, and…"

"Now, how do you know there were exactly twenty-six Mohawks?" asked Bowen. "Were you there?"

"Actually, there were twenty-eight of 'em, now that my memory is jogged," said O'Toole, knowing it would exasperate Bowen, which it did.

"Will you let him tell the story?"

"Thank you, Mr. Parker. Now, let's see, where was I? Oh, yes; those twenty-eight Mohawks were sorely outnumbered, and those that weren't killed outright were later tortured and slowly burned alive over the next few days."

"Damn, that's got to hurt," said Private Riley, grimacing and grinning at the same time.

"But that ain't all there is to the story," O'Toole reminded them.

"Do tell," said Bowen, shaking his head.

"Well, they cut the heads off all those Mohawks, all twenty-eight of 'em, and they stuck those heads on poles and set 'em up on the beach all around the island, as a warning to any other Mohawks that might want to come up this way…and that's how the island got its name."

"Interesting," said Parker.

"And that's a true story," threw in O'Toole for good measure.

"It's a story, all right," said Bowen skeptically.

"Well, I think it's interesting," said Parker. "Ain't that interesting, Metcalf?"

It seemed that Metcalf didn't hear Parker, for he just stood up and said, "I think I'll go aft and do some fishin'."

That night they all had quite a scare when the pop of muskets was heard along the western shore at around ten o'clock, and word came filtering back that some Indians and British soldiers had tried to infiltrate their lines, and so Arnold sent even more soldiers ashore to bolster their defenses, along with a couple of small-bore howitzers from off of the *Royal Savage*, which meant that nobody got much sleep that night with all the commotion.

Arnold kept them there all the next day, too, waiting for the fleet to come down the river and some of the men started questioning the wisdom of just sitting there, waiting to be overwhelmed by the British Navy.

"They ain't got no navy here," said Parker, talking more brave talk. "Besides, how are they going to get British navy ships over the rapids and down to St. John's from the St. Lawrence?"

"Well, just like those prisoners said; they could take them apart and rebuild them," answered Timmerman in that thoughtful way he had of saying things, and that wasn't what anybody wanted to hear.

"Well, I think Arnold hopes they'll come down and we'll give 'em what for, right here in the river where they can't sail around us," said Parker.

Nobody said much after that, but some of them were thinking about what Timmerman had said about taking ships apart and rebuilding them, and everybody was kind of quiet at dinnertime that evening.

At least they didn't have any more disturbances during the night and everybody more of less had a chance to get a decent night's sleep.

But the next day around ten in the morning they spotted a

couple of boats coming down the river from the direction of St. John's and the whole fleet went to quarters.

They were all standing by their loaded guns as the four bateaux kept coming toward them, and they expected at any moment to see a whole British fleet of ships-of-the-line following behind the bateaux, so it came as a great relief when those four boats fired the cannons they had mounted at their bows and then quickly turned around and headed back from whence they'd come. After remaining beside their guns for over an hour, Arnold finally had them stand down.

It was only an hour later that Arnold came around to all the ships, one at a time, to talk with each of the crews and buck them up with some words of confidence, and he reiterated that the British would not take them seriously and that their overconfidence would be their downfall. He also told them that they certainly knew they were there by now and yet they still remained holed up at St. John's, which meant that either they weren't ready for them or they were just too scared to come out and fight; and the men had a good cheer over that.

Afterwards, Arnold came over to Kinkaid and asked to meet with him in the cabin, and when they sat down next to one of the 12-pounders Arnold said, "Lieutenant, I've always thought of you as a smart and capable leader, and I have a job for you if you chose to accept it."

"For me, Sir?" said Kinkaid, surprised that he, the lowliest captain among them, would be singled out for a special task.

"By now they know exactly what we have," said Arnold, "but we know very little about their force, about their capabilities, and I aim to do something about that. Therefore, I propose to send a small party out, and I'm sending you up there with them because you know what to look for. You know your ships and what armament they're likely to have, and I want you to estimate about how many soldiers they're bringing down with them, and just do your best to have a look at what the British have at St. John's. Would you be willing to lead such a group?"

"Of course, General," said Kinkaid, and the only answer to give.

"Good. Now, a small party will be best because you'll want to remain undetected; so I wouldn't take no more than five or six men, just enough to give you a bit of firepower in case you have to fight off a patrol. Make certain they are men who you know and can trust; hearty men who can move fast, handle a musket and hatchet, and know their way about the woods. Take a telescope with you, and be sure to bring enough supplies for five days. Go far enough inland so as to avoid enemy forces along the river, and once you get up there stay only long enough to ascertain the size and capability of their ships and force of arms. Be very careful going up there, Lieutenant, but be quick and get that information back to me as soon as possible. Make sure that all in your party are informed as to what you find up there, and if you are detected, split up and come back by different routes to ensure that your information reaches me. I will send a couple of experienced men over to your ship to accompany your party, to act as guides and advisors, and I strongly suggest you listen to what they have to say. You will go tonight as soon as you are ready."

"Yes, Sir."

"And good luck to you, Lieutenant."

"Thank you, Sir."

Kinkaid had much to think about after Arnold left to give a pep talk to the crew of the next boat over, the gundalo *Philadelphia*.

Things like who he would chose to go with him, and what equipment they would bring. It also occurred to him why he had been chosen for the assignment. As the most junior officer in the fleet he was therefore the most expendable, and so he was the most reasonable and practical choice and the only choice Arnold could have made. It followed after that realization that it didn't matter what danger they might face, or even if some of them were killed or captured; the important thing was getting the information back to Arnold. All of that aside, Kinkaid also found himself wondering who the other two men would be that Arnold wanted to send with him, and that he was strongly advised to listen to.

Of one thing Kinkaid was certain; Sergeant Bowen would not come with him. Sure, he had proven himself a good sailor, and a capable soldier and leader of his marines, but Kinkaid still harbored doubts about him, and since Bowen was his first mate Kinkaid could fully justify leaving him behind.

He would take O'Toole for his knowledge of the Indians, and Parker for his strength and stamina, and then there was Goodman and Timmerman for their cool heads and common sense. He also decided he'd bring Metcalf along since he knew he was their best shot.

He then wasted no time in telling Bowen that he had been selected to lead a party up the river to St. John's and that Bowen would have to take command of the ship in his absence.

The stocky sergeant straightened right up at that and said, "You can count on me, Captain."

Kinkaid then gathered those he had chosen to go with him in the cabin, and told them, "Arnold wants to send a scouting party up to St. John's, to spy on the British base there, and he has selected our ship for that special mission." He waited for that to sink in before he continued. "Now, I took it upon myself to choose each and every one of you for your special talents and abilities, but I want you to know that I am only interested in willing volunteers since I realize this is a dangerous assignment, so if any one of you wishes to remain behind I would fully understand."

All of them quickly voiced their eagerness to go. All except for Metcalf, that is, who hesitated. But then, with all the others looking at him, he shrugged his skinny shoulders and said, "What the hell, Captain, I could use a good walk."

"That's the spirit, Sureshot," said Goodman, slapping Metcalf on the back.

And Kinkaid added, "I couldn't very well leave the best shot in the fleet behind, now, could I?"

Metcalf just grinned sheepishly.

"Now, make certain your weapons and equipment are in good order, and then draw enough provisions from Watkins to last you five days. We'll go tonight after it gets dark. And I should mention that Arnold is sending two of his men to accompany us. Any questions?"

If anyone had any questions or doubts they didn't express them, not even Metcalf.

"Good. We'll meet on the quarterdeck after dinner tonight."

It became inordinately quiet on the ship after the word got around that some of them would be going ashore that night on a special mission, and although Kinkaid found that he wasn't very hungry when dinner was served, Private Watkins had cooked up some very delicious fried catfish that the men had been hauling aboard ever since they had anchored in the river, and Kinkaid forced himself to fill his belly.

They were all sitting there on the quarterdeck as the sun began to go down behind the trees and that is when O'Toole spotted the canoe coming toward them along the row of ships. It was good-sized war canoe with only two men and a dog in it and it soon swung alongside.

One of the occupants was the Indian, Captain Cloud, daubed with war paint now, and he leaped aboard with his dog right behind him.

The other was dressed like an Indian but his long gray beard showed he was an old white man, and he looked up from the boat and asked in a squeaky voice, "Can someone give me a hand?"

Goodman reached down and helped pull the old man aboard.

Now the Indian said, "Hey, Lieutenant Kinkaid."

"Good to see you again, Captain Cloud."

The old white man wore a fringed buckskin hunting frock, leggings, and moccasins. But what really stood out was the unusual hat that he wore; the first and only skunk-skin cap that Kinkaid had ever seen, with the head of the skunk over the forehead, beady eyes and all, and the black and white tail hanging behind.

"Skaggs Holloway, at yer service," said the old man.

Both men carried a long rifle and had long knives and tomahawks in their belts.

"So who all's goin'?" asked Holloway.

"I am, and these five men here," said Kinkaid.

Skaggs looked everyone over like he was judging livestock and then he said, "Well, I hope yer all fast walkers. But we're burnin' moonlight, so let's get goin' if'n we're goin'."

XII

The Scouting Party

A tiny crescent of a moon hovered over the lake and shimmered on the surface as the party set out, all eight of them in the big canoe, and soon their paddles were dipping silently into the black river as they made their way past the last two gundalos and headed toward the shore.

It wasn't long before the canoe slid up onto the sandy beach and they all leaped out with their weapons and packs. Then Skaggs then had them all gather together at the edge of the trees.

"Lieutenant, you and your men follow Captain Cloud and I'll bring up the rear. Just be quiet and keep movin'. And if'n we run into anybody, don't even think about fightin' it out. Just scatter and make your way back here. Understand?"

Everybody nodded and then Skaggs said, "Let's go, then."

Captain Cloud crouched low as he crept through the bushes that lined the riverbank, and after shouldering his pack with the heavy telescope in it Kinkaid followed behind him as they all entered the pitch black forest where the moon sent shafts of silvery light down through the branches of the tall pines.

They hadn't gone more than fifty yards into the forest when Kinkaid turned to make sure that the others were following behind him, and when he turned back he didn't see the Indian.

Disoriented, Kinkaid stopped suddenly, causing Goodman to run into him and mutter, "Oh, excuse me, Sir."

The Indian appeared from behind the tree right in front of Kinkaid and crouching low he whispered, "No talk. Get down."

They all crouched low and nobody moved, except that Skaggs Holloway came up and listened to what the Indian had to say.

"Everybody stay put," whispered Skaggs as Captain Cloud went on alone. "They got patrols out."

They all waited there for six or seven minutes until the Indian came back and said, "Patrol pass. We go now."

And off he went again, with Kinkaid right behind him.

The tall pines soon gave way to a mixed forest of maple, oak and hemlock and the feeble light of the moon provided enough visibility to follow the Indian as he stepped up the pace.

Soon they were heading uphill through the forest and the men starting slipping and sliding because the ground under the leaves here was wet and muddy from natural springs that bubbled out of the side of the hill.

But Captain Cloud was patient with them and kept halting so that they could catch up, and before long they made it to the top of the hill where the land was flat and relatively even, although there was no trail to speak of and they had to watch out for exposed roots, fallen logs and jutting rocks that tripped them and banged their legs.

Then the Indian took them through a bramble bush and the thorns tore at their clothes and cut their face and arms and legs, and by the time they reached the other side of the hill they were all so exhausted and beaten and bruised and breathing hard that Captain Cloud let them rest for a few minutes.

"You men lead easy life on ship too much," said the Indian, meaning they were out of shape.

"I suppose so," Kinkaid had to agree, and it surprised him that the old man Holloway seemed to be none the worse for wear.

It was Metcalf who expressed what everybody else was thinking when he blurted out, "I wonder where we are?"

For once, Kinkaid thought Metcalf had a point, for he knew that he would never be able to make it back to the ship on his own right then. He was lost and he knew it. Another thing that bothered him was that the dog seemed to be leading the way, or else it knew where the Indian wanted to go before he went there. And it was all a bit unsettling.

They soon started out again and they hiked all night through an ever changing wilderness, sometimes through open maple forests, or through dense spruce and hemlock, and other times across bogs where the ground tried to suck their shoes off, and by morning they found themselves at the edge of a marsh where a line of willows hung over a glade in the forest.

"All stay here," Captain Cloud told them. "I go looksee." And off he went, the dog out front.

After the Indian had gone, Skaggs said, "Stay quiet and no fires, but eat if'n you're hungry, and then get some sleep. I'll keep watch."

Everyone took off their packs, and Goodman and Metcalf ate some of the hardtack that Watkins had provided them, but so tired was everyone that before long they were all wrapped up in their blankets and asleep, all except for

Holloway.

Kinkaid thought he'd surely fall asleep after hiking all night over rough terrain, but his mind was too active and he starting thinking that they were probably lost and that is why the Indian went ahead without them, to find out where they were, and after listening to birds singing in the forest for a while he stood up from his blanket and went over to where Skaggs Holloway sat on a log with his rifle cradled easily in his arms.

Not knowing if he was welcome or not, Kinkaid asked, "That's quite a gun you have there, Mr. Holloway."

"It's a rifle."

"A rifle?"

"Means the barrel is grooved so it spins the ball," explained Skaggs. "Makes for greater accuracy. Why, I can shoot the eye out of a turkey at a hundred yards with this; 'course my eyes ain't what they used to be."

"Where did you get it?"

"Traded it for a dozen sable pelts from some hunter from Kentuck, down on his luck. Yippee, did ya catch that rhyme?"

"I certainly did."

"That's why I call her Kentuck," he said proudly, holding the rifle out. "Here, try her on for size."

Kinkaid took the long weapon and hefted it up to his shoulder and aimed along the barrel.

"It does have a nice feel to it."

"Don't it?"

Now that Kinkaid had the man talking he handed the rifle back and asked, "Are we lost?"

"Lost?" said Skaggs like he'd been insulted. "I doubt that. Nope, when we leave here we'll go right through that cranberry patch over yonder. Then we'll go straight for about twenty miles, until we come to a slow-movin' brook. And that's where we'll turn a bit to the northeast and follow that brook right down into a beautiful valley. St. John's and the river is only two miles from there. Don't worry, Lieutenant; we'll get you there."

"So I take it you've been up this way before."

"Sure have."

"I wasn't worried," said Kinkaid. "Just feeling a bit disoriented."

"Well, that's understandable."

"It seems like the dog is leading the way."

"I can see as how you might think that."

Half a dozen blue jays had landed high up in a pine tree over their heads and were squawking and scolding the humans they had spotted down below, and with no further explanation from Skaggs explaining how the dog knew where they were going better than anyone else, Kinkaid changed his tack and said, "You don't seem like the average soldier to me. Mr. Holloway."

"I ain't no soldier," said Skaggs sharply. "I'm hired on as a scout and a hunter. Never have been; never will be no soldier, nosiree. I hate the army. Why, it's filled with nothin' but dirty, smelly, noisy fools…for the most part." Skaggs especially hated the way that young officers liked to lord it over their men, but he wouldn't mention that to Kinkaid, a young officer himself.

"Arnold is a soldier," Kinkaid reminded him.

"Well, Arnold is the only one I ever met who knew what he was doin'. No offense, Lieutenant, but I even hate workin' for the army. But now I got no choice. They got the Indians so stirred up that it ain't hardly safe for a soul to be out in the woods by his lonesome these days, not even if he's just mindin' his own business. I just hope this war is over soon so I can get back to my trap line and make an honest livin' again."

"So you're a trapper by trade."

"Among other things," said Skaggs without mentioning what they were.

"When do you think the Indian will return?"

Skaggs turned his head at the lilting song of a wood thrush, and then he imitated the song and said, "I believe he's back now."

Sure enough the Indian appeared out the patch of cranberry bushes that Skaggs had said they'd be heading through after he returned, and he came over and said something to Skaggs in his Indian language and then the men were awakened and told they'd all better have something to eat and so they all did that.

The Indian and Skaggs shared what Kinkaid guessed must have been pemmican, for it looked to be like a bar of grains and dried fruit, held together with something sticky like honey or molasses. Then they started out again, right through the cranberry patch.

They covered a lot of ground that day and the Indian finally let them sleep for about four hours that night, but then had them moving even before the sun came up and he kept them moving all day and again into the evening and by now they were all flagging.

Even the old man, Skaggs, was breathing hard and looked about ready to keel over. The only one who seemed to take it as well as the Indian was Metcalf, although he constantly looked nervous and kept turning his head this way and that, expecting to see hordes of Indians coming out of the forest, guessed Kinkaid.

It was the third day and the Indian led them off at first light. They moved slowly at first, with the dog still leading the way; at least that is how it appeared to Kinkaid. And then they hit a deer trail that seemed to begin at the edge of a large stand of tall pines. The trail was soft and deeply cut into the loam under the pines as if it had been used by animals for a very long time and that's when the Indian started jogging.

Kinkaid jogged behind him and the others were forced to keep up and soon they were all panting from the effort, though it scarcely seemed to affect the Indian as he lopped along, hopping over the occasional root or fallen log, or ducking under a low branch here and there just like a deer would.

Every now and then Kinkaid would see the dog way out in front of them, but mostly it was out of sight and he kept wondering how the dog and the Indian kept track of one another. Once in a while the Indian would get too far ahead of Kinkaid, and every time he did that Kinkaid would contemplate saying something, but then the Indian would turn around and notice and then he would patiently wait for him to catch up.

Finally, Goodman started to cough, a loud, wracking cough that he couldn't seem to stop and so they rested for about half an hour at the edge of the stand of tall pines where there were hundreds of little pine trees just starting out where somebody had once cleared that area for the straight trees.

It was about five in the afternoon and the Indian and his dog had gone up ahead, as usual, but he came running back in a hurry only a few minutes later and said, "All be quiet and lay down in trees."

And so they all hid among the little pine trees and it wasn't long before they heard the jangling of a harness, and soon enough Kinkaid could see that a wagon with half a dozen men on it was coming up along the edge of the trees where there must have been a road.

They all froze as the wagon went by about fifty yards away and after it passed the Indian took them across the road and down a slight incline and through an apple orchard where they stopped along the bank of a slow moving stream. The sun was going down now.

Skaggs explained, "The British get their straight logs from that pine forest back there. We're only about three miles from St. John's now, so keep extra quiet and keep your wits about you."

The brook meandered through the apple orchard and then broke into some small rapids as it started down a hill through the woods, and just as it began to grow quite dark the brook brought them to a meadow that looked out over a beautiful valley where there were some farms and more orchards, and some cows out in the fields. That is when Captain Cloud stopped and said, "I go with Kinkaid now. Others wait here."

"Well, it's up to you now, Lieutenant," said Skaggs. "Captain Cloud will take you down the brook where it runs right into the river by their main docks. You should be able to get a good look at them from there at first light. Oh, and I was supposed to give you this."

Skaggs reached into his frock and pulled out a paper and a pencil and handed it to Kinkaid.

"You're supposed to write down all that you see."

"Thank you," was all he could think to say, so nervous was he. It was time to do or die, and fulfill the task that he had been brought up here to do, to give Arnold an accurate picture of what they faced.

"Good luck to you, Sir," said O'Toole.

"We'll be waiting right here for you," Skaggs reminded

him. "Don't stay any longer than you need to."

The Indian motioned to the dog and it sat next to Skaggs and remained there as Kinkaid followed Captain Cloud along the brook. They made good time, too, in the dark, although they had to slog through a couple of marshy areas and Kinkaid's feet were soaking wet by the time they saw the Richelieu River sparking in the moonlight through the trees and they could smell wood smoke, and that is when the Indian said, "We hide here until light."

In spite of their forced march and lack of sleep, Kinkaid was too excited to sleep right away, knowing how close they were to enemy lines, and so he asked the Indian, "How is it that you came to work for General Arnold?"

"I meet Arnold in town called Danbury. I there to trade furs. He on his way to big lake. White man say he take furs in trade for rifle. But then he take my furs and then give me old jack knife. When I complain they beat me, but Arnold put stop to that. He make them give me rifle, too. When he ask me if I scout for him, I say yes."

"Do you have a family?"

"Wife die; white man's disease."

Sorry he had asked, Kinkaid stopped asking the Indian questions, and with no conversation coming from the Indian, Kinkaid wrapped his wool blanket about himself and tried to get some sleep.

But it wasn't easy, for it was cold and he shivered all night with his wet feet, and at first light he got up and moved a bit closer to the river.

Captain Cloud followed close behind him through a misty fog, until they came to a tall white spruce and the Indian said, "Good place for looksee," and pointed up the tree.

Kinkaid placed his pack and musket on the ground and after looping the cord of his telescope around his neck he began to climb the tree, and it was relatively easy to do because the branches were regularly spaced and it wasn't long before he began to see the tops of some buildings and tall masts revealed to him in the early morning light over the lingering fog.

He found a good spot a little over halfway up the tree where a branch had broken off during some storm, affording a clear view, and he only had to wait half an hour or so before the fog began to blow away with the light breeze and more of the town and harbor was revealed to him. And what he saw made him gasp in awe.

He could see, even without the telescope, that the place was a beehive of activity, even that early in the morning, with men coming and going, and with horse-drawn carts coming up to the docks, all piled high with provisions of every kind; crates of fruits and vegetables, barrels of salted meat, rounds of cheese, and even livestock.

But what really caught Kinkaid's eye were the ships he saw at the harbor with their brightly colored flags and pennants blowing in the light breeze, at least thirty in all. At least four of them were real ships like the kind that went to sea and crossed oceans, and each one of them was larger than anything Arnold had, proving once and for all the rumors of the British taking large ships apart and reassembling them here.

One ship in particular looked like a small frigate with its three masts, square-rigged sails and yellow and black-checkered hull, with at least ten gunports running down her side, and when he took a closer look through the telescope he found that he could read her name on a plaque at her stern; the *Inflexible*. And now Kinkaid recalled the names of those other ships that the British prisoners had described and he knew that they hadn't been exaggerating after all, for they were right in front of him; two large schooners armed with at least a dozen guns each, one called the *Maria* and the other the *Carleton*. There was also something that Kinkaid had never seen before; a long barge of some kind, with a ketch rig. It was a monstrous thing; flat-sided and squared-off at the bow. It was at least ninety feet long and had a wide beam of over thirty feet, where sat a dozen large bore cannons, half of them massive 24-pounders. She was a veritable monster of a gun platform, showing that the British could be ingenious as well. And now he realized that this must be the vessel they referred to as a radeau. What had they called her; *Thunderer*? Not only that but all those ships seemed to be manned by real sailors and officers of the Royal Navy, for Kinkaid recognized their uniforms.

Behind those four large ships were dozens upon dozens of smaller craft, much like Arnold's gondolas, each armed with a single heavy cannon at the bow as well as having swivel guns mounted alongside. And farther up the way were so many bateaux that Kinkaid lost count as the line of them vanished around the corner of the river.

So astonished was Kinkaid that he at first forgot about his paper and pencil, but then he quickly began to write down all that was before him. As he was finishing his list he looked up to find that a large contingent of troops was marching from the town to the docks. And then, yes, they were boarding the ships. Hundreds of soldiers kept pouring out of the streets of St. John's, and it could only mean one thing; the British were about to come down the lake in force.

Kinkaid scrambled back down the tree, and this time it was Captain Cloud who had a difficult time keeping up as they hurried back to the spot along the brook where the others were anxiously waiting.

Though they were all eager to leave the area Kinkaid

hurriedly made two more copies of what he had written down and gave one copy to O'Toole and the other to Timmerman. He also read aloud everything on his list so that they all might have an idea as to what he had seen, to make certain that in case anything happened to him it would be more than likely that somebody would get the information back to Arnold, and the looks on their faces when they heard it all was sobering. Even the normally optimistic Jack Parker looked worried by the time he finished reading the list.

As they started out they had a scare when that wagon of men that they had seen the evening before came back down the road piled high with long straight logs, and it was a close thing as they all took cover under the small pine trees again.

They all froze and huddled quietly under the fir boughs as the wagon passed. But then Metcalf got curious and foolishly looked up, and that is when one of the men sitting on top of the logs in the back of the wagon spotted him and gave a shout.

Now they all jumped up and went running into the tall pines as somebody fired a musket, but they were all soon running along the trail that was deeply cut into the loam and nobody seemed to be pursuing them.

At least it didn't seem that those men on the wagon were pursuing them, because after a while the Indian had them stop and told them to wait for him as he went back to check, and when he returned he said, "They no come."

The words came as a great relief and Kinkaid saw that the others were smiling, like they were thinking it was all a big adventure or game of some kind, whereby they had outfoxed the British.

But then it quickly occurred to Kinkaid that those men with the wagon would certainly report their sighting to someone in authority when they reached the town. It also occurred to him that it had been his own fault that they had been detected, for he should have waited until they were deep in the forest before stopping to make copies of the information. Therefore, he didn't mind so much when Captain Cloud kept them running hard all that day and right past the noon hour, and when Metcalf complained that he was getting weak from hunger the Indian told him, "Eat on run."

Which is what they did, and all of them were soon munching on hardtack or pemmican as they kept running. At one point in the afternoon Goodman started coughing again and that is when Captain Cloud finally relented and let them rest for ten minutes.

That is when Kinkaid asked him, "Do you think they will come after us?"

Captain Cloud nodded and said, "They take better trail along river; get ahead of us, easy. Set ambush."

He said it matter-of-factly and Kinkaid knew he was right and it sent a chill up his spine, for now his foolish mistake loomed much larger and he began to wonder if he would be the cause of their deaths.

The others heard what the Indian had said, too, and now it didn't seem like a game anymore, and the frightened look on Metcalf's face, bordering on panic, was something none of them would ever forget.

Captain Cloud kept them moving all through the night, although at a slower pace, and at first light he began to jog again, but it was no use, for by now they were all huffing and puffing, barely able to walk fast and the Indian had no choice but to wait for them all as they staggered along.

They kept moving all that day and by late afternoon made it back to the hill that they had gone over the first day. It was a struggle to get up the hill for the men were utterly exhausted by now. They had had very little nourishment to sustain them and they'd slept very little, but they knew that safety was only a couple of miles away.

Captain Cloud took them through the same bramble bush and then led them to the top of the hill where the ground was relatively flat but covered in fallen logs, roots and jutting rocks and their progress slowed considerably, but never once did the Indian flag in his vigilance, and Skaggs Holloway was heroic as he brought up the rear and kept encouraging the stragglers to keep up.

It was as they were about to come down on the other side of the hill when Captain Cloud stopped them.

The dog, Little Scout, was about halfway down the hill and it stood there as if frozen, looking into the trees beyond and Captain Cloud said to Kinkaid, "They wait for us there. I go looksee."

When the Indian came back a half hour later Kinkaid asked him, "How many?"

"Enough."

"Can we get around them?"

"No."

"Then what will we do?"

Captain Cloud went down to where his dog stood and said something to him, whereupon the dog started running off to the right and was soon lost from sight.

When the Indian came back up the hill he said, "I send Little Scout for help."

By now the others had caught up and they gathered together behind a cluster of rocks near the top of the hill, and Kinkaid had to tell them, "Looks like we've been cut off."

"Well, how do you know for sure?" asked Goodman.

Captain Cloud said, "Many Indians and soldiers between

us and river. When they know we not come down, they will come up."

"We'd better prepare for them," said Kinkaid.

"Well, do you think we should surrender?" asked Metcalf, and they all looked at him like he was crazy.

"We can't surrender," Kinkaid told him. "We've got to get that information to Arnold. But if you want to give yourself up, go ahead."

Even Metcalf must have felt shame for suggesting such a thing, for he shrugged his skinny shoulders and said, "No, I guess I'll stick with you fellows."

No one said much after that as they all spread out alongside the hill and each found a position behind a rock or a fallen log and did their best to improve it by moving more logs or rocks in front and beside them.

Kinkaid and the Indian were in the middle, with Skaggs Holloway, Timmerman and Goodman holding the left flank while O'Toole, Jack Parker, and Metcalf held the right, and once they were all satisfied with their defensive positions they did their best to settled down and relax.

"Mind if I smoke, Sir?" asked O'Toole.

"I don't see why not," said Kinkaid, "if they already know we're here."

The nervous Metcalf asked, "Do you think we have a chance, Lieutenant?"

"With you as our best shot?" said Kinkaid, trying to bolster the boy's courage. "We also hold the high ground and have the advantage of defending."

He knew as he spoke that he was trying to focus on the positive even as he realized that their small group could easily be outflanked and overrun by a larger force.

"And we have the sun behind us," mentioned Skaggs, trying to help.

It was true; the sun was just beginning to set through the bare branches of the trees behind them when the Indian gave one of his bird calls and everyone froze.

"They come," said Captain Cloud. "Hold fire until close."

They all crouched low behind their respective positions and waited for the inevitable, and it wasn't long before the rustle of leaves could be heard down the hill. And then they started seeing quick movements as soldiers and Indians dashed from behind one tree to another, all brandishing rifles or muskets, and with tomahawks flashing.

Kinkaid was in the middle, in a little depression with a large flat rock in front of him that he could fire over, and he lay with his chest on the rock, aiming his musket down the hill. As the enemy drew toward the bottom of the hill he picked out one man, an Indian whose head was painted black and his chest red, and although he was aware that there must have been at least twenty or more men heading through the forest in their direction, he tried to concentrate on aiming at that one Indian's red chest as he flitted from tree to tree.

Kinkaid waited for the Indian to come out from behind the last tree, intending to shoot him in the chest, when Metcalf's musket went off just before Kinkaid squeezed the trigger on his gun, and when he looked through the smoke of his discharge he saw nothing and knew that he had missed.

"I got one!" he heard Metcalf shout, but then all was bedlam as the hill erupted in musket and rifle fire, the air filled with puffs of dirty gray smoke, and with Indians yipping and hollering.

Now it was a question of firing accurately and then frantically reloading, and the deadly exchange went on for ten minutes as bullets pinged off the rocks and thudded into logs and zipped through the branches over their heads, and at first it seemed like the enemy was being suppressed, for they rarely saw a target.

But then they began leaping from tree to tree again, and so fast that one scarcely had the time to aim before they would take cover again, and they began to move inexorably up the hill.

"They're coming up on the left!" shouted Skaggs.

"On the right, too!" yelled Metcalf.

But Kinkaid didn't have time to look in either direction for he was shocked to see at least thirty men running straight up the hill toward them, most of them Indians, and they were yipping and screaming like banshees.

They were being rushed from three sides and Kinkaid felt a cold wave of fear grip his body and nervous system, making his muscles seem frozen, and it was with the greatest effort that he aimed his musket and fired into the group of them and saw a soldier pitch backward when his bullet smacked into the man's neck.

As second later he heard Goodman cry out, "I'm shot!"

"Can you still fight?" asked Skaggs.

"Yes!" yelled Goodman resolutely.

Kinkaid was hunched behind the big flat rock reloading his musket as he heard the shuffling of leaves as the enemy came ever closer up the hill and the others did their best to keep shooting at them. But it dawned on him that the enemy would soon be swarming over their position, close enough to use their tomahawks.

That is when he thought he heard a volley of fire farther down the hill, and after he had reloaded he looked over the rock and saw that the enemy had hesitated, for they too had heard the volley behind them.

Then one of the Indians yelped and the whole group ran off through the trees to the left, vanishing silently into the forest.

Kinkaid leaped over to where Goodman lay. He was on his back with an arm across his chest. Kinkaid lifted the arm and saw a bloody wound just under Goodman's left collar bone.

"How are you doing?" Kinkaid asked the big man.

"I've been better," said Goodman gamely.

It was only a few minutes later that the rustling of leaves could be heard again at the bottom of the hill and when Kinkaid looked he was relieved to see a bunch of men in buckskin and homespun all carrying rifles and coming up the hill for he knew right away that they were some of Arnold's riflemen.

And there came Little Scout, running up the hill as fast as he could fly and he ran right up to Captain Cloud and jumped on his chest, knocking him down and licking his face.

"Damn, are we glad to see you boys," said Skaggs as he stood up from behind his log.

Everybody had been too busy during the fight to notice that Captain Cloud had never fired his rifle at the Indians attacking them.

XIII

Council of War

When they reached the bottom of the hill Kinkaid looked for the man he had shot, but found nothing but some leaves spotted with blood. In fact, not a single body could be found, and Metcalf was sure he had killed at least two, showing that the Indians were very careful about leaving anybody behind, especially their dead.

Goodman had been badly wounded but was treated by Arnold's physician, and after he removed the bullet O'Toole placed a poultice of herbs over the wound to keep it from festering and to speed the healing, but Goodman would be bedridden in the cabin for at least a week and so he had to relinquish his role of gun captain of the 18-pounder to Timmerman.

The fight on the hill had been a close call and Kinkaid knew that they had only been saved at the last moment by Arnold's riflemen. It seems Arnold had anticipated that his scouting party might be ambushed upon their return and had sent a whole company of riflemen out to be of assistance. Then, when Captain Cloud's dog showed up on the beach without the Indian they knew that something was amiss and were able to drive off the enemy party in the nick of time.

The crew of the *Trumbull* were more than interested in hearing about their mates' scout up the river and were especially keen to learn the details of their fight on the hillside, especially since they'd all heard the sound of the muskets popping and feared for their lives, and so Metcalf was in his glory as he told them the story of how they had expected the ambush and then about how he had shot and killed at least two of the enemy, claiming the glory of being the first among them to have spilled the blood of their enemy. He even carved a couple of neat notches on the stock of his musket to keep track of his tally of those who had fallen to his marksmanship.

While Kinkaid felt a slight wobbling in his knees whenever he thought about how close they'd all come to being killed and scalped, he felt pretty good about his conduct under fire, for although he had been badly frightened when he realized they were cut off, once the shooting began he found that he had been cool and collected and did what had to be done. He also knew that he had killed a man, a man he did not know. It was the first man he had ever killed, but unlike Metcalf he could not gloat over the fact but even felt a twinge of guilt, although he also found that he could justify the deed because they were at war and it was either kill or be killed.

Kinkaid delivered his written list of all that he had seen at St. John's to Arnold personally in his cabin aboard the *Royal Savage* and he could not help but see the look of grave concern on Arnold's face when he read it, for it proved once and for all that the British had more and bigger ships, more and heavier cannons, and was manned by a plethora of skilled seamen and gunners, not to mention the army of soldiers the fleet carried with it.

Even so Arnold gave Kinkaid a smile and tried to make light of it by saying, "Good work, Lieutenant. Now we know what we're up against."

Kinkaid also learned from Arnold that the British had sent more boats down the river while he was gone on his scout, and that the British hoped to lure the American fleet farther up the river where they no doubt had set up an ambush for them, but that Arnold had refrained from taking the bait.

Kinkaid also heard that when the *Boston*'s crew had gone ashore for firewood they had been attacked by a party of Indians led by a British lieutenant named Scott who had called for the Americans to surrender. They refused and managed to scramble back aboard their boats but not before three of the *Boston*'s crew were killed and six were wounded, and it was thought that this was the same group that had waited to waylay Kinkaid's scouting party.

And even while Kinkaid was still meeting with Arnold a Captain Hoover from a regiment of Continentals that were camping ashore came and reported to him that they had been hearing the sound of axes in the forest on either side of where the fleet was anchored, and Arnold surmised that the British were in the process of constructing batteries with which to cannonade their ships and catch them in a crossfire.

Therefore, Kinkaid was not surprised when less than an hour after returning to the *Trumbull* he received the order from Arnold that the fleet would set sail immediately. Kinkaid also realized that it was in part because of the information he had provided, that Arnold must have felt less than comfortable having them simply anchored there in the river, just waiting for the British fleet to show up, and that a change in tactics was called for.

And so they sailed back down the lake all that day and into the night, and by the next morning Arnold had brought them back to Valcour Island, halfway between Ticonderoga and the British base of St. John's, close to the New York shore.

There they also met another of their gundalos, the *New York*, coming up from Ticonderoga, and with it came a message from General Gates, asking Arnold what the cannon fire had been all about the week before.

Of course Arnold knew that Gates had merely heard their salute when the *Lee* and the *New Jersey* had come up to join them and, somewhat embarrassed, he ignored the question, especially since they were short of powder and that the salute had been a waste of it, but Arnold did write a letter back to Gates asking for more ships, more guns, more cannonballs and powder, more men, especially real sailors, and that some clothing and blankets would be much appreciated.

Valcour Island was two miles long from north to south and was a mile across, with a rocky shoreline and covered in tall pine trees and gnarled cedar and spruce, and most of the color along the hills was gone now since the leaves had fallen in preparation for the coming winter.

It was late in the afternoon by the time they had passed down the eastern side of the island and Arnold had his ships drop anchor at the southern tip. He then immediately called for a council of war.

And now Kinkaid found himself standing on the deck of the *Royal Savage*, amidships, and in the midst of all the other captains.

There was Captain Hawley, and Smith of the *Enterprise*, and Seamon of the *Revenge,* and Premier of the *Liberty*. And there was Davis of the row galley *Lee*, and Warner of the *Congress*. All of the gundalo captains were there as well; Ulmer of the *Spitfire*, and Rue of the *Philadelphia*, as well as Sumner, Grant, Grimes, Mansfield, Lee and Simonds, and they were all of them a grim but determined lot.

Skaggs Holloway and Captain Cloud were there; too, both leaning against the after stern rail, smoking their pipes, with the dog, Little Scout, at their feet, and both men gave Kinkaid a nod of recognition which Kinkaid returned.

Now here came Arnold out of the cabin. Always a careful dresser, he wore his best uniform for the occasion and made a heroic figure as he climbed up the ladder and stood upon the quarterdeck.

Knowing the power of the enemy fleet that he faced, Arnold had thought about how he might delay or even defeat them, and he knew now what had to be done and had chosen this spot to do it in. And though he was a bold and decisive leader, and once he made his mind up about something he'd likely follow through in spite of all opposition, he was no tyrant and had learned that his fellows and colleagues-in-arms tended to be intimidated by him and so he decided to call a council of war to explain his plans to his fellow officers and help make them believe that he was seeking their advice and opinions.

"Let there be no mistaking what we are about, Gentlemen," began Arnold in that sonorous voice of his. "Our chief aim has always been and remains now to delay the British. Our show of force almost two months ago served us well in that regard, for when they saw what we had on the lake they knew they would have to build more ships to oppose us. But now I believe they are ready and we may expect them with the next north wind.

"I have considered our strengths and weaknesses and have concluded that we cannot meet the British as an equal out on the lake where they will have the weather gauge and be able to maneuver against us piecemeal. Therefore, what I propose is that we take our fleet into the bay there, formed between

Valcour Island and the shore. In this way we will be hidden from their advance as they come down the lake. Only once past the island will our position be revealed to them. They will then have to buck the prevailing north wind to come up to us, losing much of their cohesion and discipline, for some of their ships will tack better than others and they will necessarily run afoul of one another in their eagerness to engage us. Remember, they don't take us seriously; they never have, and this shall be to our advantage."

Kinkaid watched the men as they listened to Arnold speak, and he could tell that they liked what he was saying.

"By forming a crescent in the bay there we will be able to meet each of their ships in turn as they come up to us with our full weight of cannon. And that is the key, gentlemen; our ability to bring every one of our guns to bear while they can only employ a few of theirs against us until they draw nearer, and by then we will have given them a severe mauling. What say you; are you with me, captains?"

Captain Smith of the sloop *Enterprise* was the first to speak up, saying, "It is a good plan, and I am for it."

This brought more than a few "Hear, hears," from the others.

"What if they come down the channel behind us?" asked Captain Seamon of the schooner *Revenge*.

"A good question, but I would say they will not, and for two reasons. First, they will not come carefully, but in haste. Their commanders know that the hour is late. Second, they will come with the knowledge that they are stronger than us. And this will preclude them from coming between the island and the shore, for most of their principal vessels will be ships, with drafts too deep to chance a run down the channel where there are likely to be rocks and shoals to tear out their bottoms."

"I think you are right, General," said Captain Premier of the *Liberty*. But then he added, "I too think it is as good a plan as any, but what happens once they have all come up to us?"

"You are thinking ahead, Captain Premier," said Arnold, "and that is a good thing. What I can tell you is that our best effort must be in the beginning, when they are jockeying to come up us, for their captains will be eager, all wishing to be the first to engage us. If we anchor our vessels fore and aft so that our broadsides oppose their bows, we will maul them as they come up. Of course it is possible, even probable, that we will be eventually outnumbered, for I must tell you that their vessels will be many, of that I have no doubt, and bigger, too. But remember also, that it does not matter so much what happens to our ships; no, not even to ourselves so much. What matters is that we delay them, gentlemen; give them such a beating that they will be unable to continue their advance down the lake, and in this I am certain we will succeed, for our gunners are well-trained and second to none by now."

No one said a word after that, but all considered what Arnold had said. They valued his judgment and were all well familiar with General Arnold's honesty by now, his quick and clear assessment of any situation, and they appreciated this about him, admitting that they would most likely be overwhelmed as the battle went on, but he also stoked their courage by reminding them that delay was the real purpose of all of their efforts in building and fighting this fleet, and he showed them his confidence by mentioning the skill of their gunnery, taught in most cases by Arnold himself.

And now he said, "Good. Then if we are in agreement, let us all return to our commands and form ourselves in the bay; sort ourselves out in as formidable a line as possible so that we may present our heaviest guns to the enemy. I shall come around to all of the vessels and make sure each and every one of us is in the best position possible before nightfall. And let me say that once the battle is engaged we will remain flexible as to any opportunities that may present, even for the possibility of a running battle down the lake through their confused and battered ranks, for we have plenty of wide and open water before us to the south, so keep your axes handy. And of course we shall also consider our options for saving ourselves."

"It is a good plan, General," agreed Captain Hawley of the *Royal Savage*, "and I would only propose that we send out one of our vessels to keep a reconnaissance of the lake and a close eye to the north, to give us time to prepare."

"Excellent idea," said Arnold, not that he hadn't already thought of it himself, "and since I shall be transferring to the *Congress*, I propose that it be you and your vessel, Captain Hawley."

"I heartily accept the honor, Sir."

"I also need a ship to go back to Fort Ticonderoga to deliver my dispatch to General Gates and to bring us as much supplies as are available there, for there is no telling how long it may take our British friends to show up."

This brought a few chuckles.

"And since I know there will no volunteers, I will ask Captain Premier of the *Liberty* if he would be so kind as to fulfill this most important duty."

"I would be honored, General," said Captain Premier.

There were also a number of sick that would have to go back, but Arnold did not mention this, but said, "Very well. Let us make ready, then."

The fleet then formed itself in a curved line half a mile across the southern end of the bay formed between Valcour

Island and the New York shore, and it wasn't long before Arnold came aboard each and every vessel, to make sure each was properly anchored both fore and aft, and to ensure that the greatest weight of broadside would meet the enemy fleet as they came up into the bay.

He also had the crews of the ships go ashore and cut pine boughs to line their bulwarks as a means to help repel boarders and to provide a bit more protection from small arms fire, and they toiled at this all that day and into the evening and now all the ships looked like floating islands of pine, hemlock, balsam and spruce.

A cold rain fell that night, driven by a hard wind and those men not on duty huddled below while those on the deck sat wrapped in blankets and turned their faces away from the wind. The wind and rain continued right into the morning as all the crews waited aboard their respective vessels, and it was hard to stay warm and dry as they waited for the British fleet to find them, and they all knew that it was only a matter of time before they would have to do battle.

It was after their noon meal when Metcalf was heard to say, "Well, I wish they'd hurry up and come, if they're comin'."

"Why are you in such an all-fired hurry?" asked somebody.

"Because he's eager to add to his tally," said another.

"That's right; he wants a few more notches on the stock of his musket," said somebody else, and everybody knew that Metcalf was afraid, and that he had exaggerated his telling of the fight along the hill. They even doubted that he had killed a single man, which went to show that being a braggart only went against a man, even when he had a real story to tell of bravery and resolve in the face of the enemy.

"It's just that I don't like all this waitin'," said Metcalf, and they could all agree with that.

"You should take up the pipe," said O'Toole, sitting comfortably with the smoke of his own fancy pipe curling around his head. "It helps a man relax."

"I did try smoking a pipe once," said Metcalf, "but it near choked me to death."

"Well, you have to give it a chance, but then there are some who are too sensitive for tobacky."

"It's probably too late now, anyway," said Jack Parker, giving O'Toole a wink.

"Too late for what?" asked Metcalf.

"Too late to take up smoking," said Parker. "Haven't you been following the conversation?"

"Hey, what's that smell?" asked Goodman.

"That's those rotten potatoes," said Timmerman. "I told you most all of our potatoes are rotten."

"Yet the cook keeps feedin' 'em to us," said Metcalf.

"And you keep eatin' 'em."

"Well, a rotten potato is better than no potato."

"I don't know about that," said Goodman. "I can't stomach them any more."

"Which is why he's startin' to mash them up with carrots, so's we won't notice."

"Well, I notice."

"I just wish we still had some coffee."

"Yeah, I'm gettin' sick of drinking burnt oatmeal water."

"Is that what we've been drinking?"

"For a week now; didn't you notice?"

"Hell, I wish we had some beer," said Sergeant Bowen, breaking everyone's chain of thought, for in spite of their strict rationing, their last barrel had been emptied the day they had left the Richelieu.

They were not only being fed rotten potatoes by this time,

but they were also getting very low on food of all kinds. In fact, they were all at about the limits of their endurance by now, and it must have been terrible for those men assigned to the relatively open gundalos, having to brave the cold and the wet and the wind with little shelter and inadequate clothing, and now many of the men aboard the ships were coming down with fevers and chills and each ship that left with dispatches for General Gates also had a number of men aboard who had to be sent back with the ague, diminishing the manpower of the fleet.

On the 6th of October the row galley *Washington*, under the command of John Thatcher, came up and joined the fleet, bringing their total of dangerous gunboats to four and eliciting some cheers from the other ships as she took her station near the middle of their formation in the bay. Kinkaid halfheartedly joined in the cheering, but knowing what they faced he knew she would not tip the balance in their favor.

Also aboard her was a man who Gates had appointed to be the fleet's second in command, General David Waterbury, who had done such a fine job of overseeing the construction of most of Arnold's ships. But of even more interest to the crews was that the *Washington* had brought up a barrel of rum for every ship in the fleet and now they even had something to celebrate with. Though she also brought news that the *Gates* was still unfinished because of illness among the builders and had yet to come up to Ticonderoga from Skenesboro for her final fitting out.

That night was colder than the night before and it even began to snow a little, and some of the men started talking hopefully about how it was probably already too late in the season for the British to launch their assault down the lake, but Kinkaid thought that that was mostly wishful thinking.

The wind shifted from the north on the 8th of October to

coming from out of the south and they all knew that any British fleet would not be able to buck that wind and so they all tried to relax a bit.

The wind continued to blow from out of the south until the early morning hours of the 11th and then it shifted once again and blew from the north, increasing the tension around the fleet that had been anchored in the relatively sheltered bay of Valcour Island for almost three weeks now, for they all remembered that Arnold had told them that the British fleet would probably be coming down the lake with the next north wind.

XIV

The Battle of Valcour Island

It was almost eight o'clock in the morning when they all heard the dull boom of a single cannon.

"What's that?" asked Sergeant Bowen.

"It must be the guard boat that Arnold sent out at first light," said O'Toole, who had had the early morning watch and had seen the boat go out.

Kinkaid went up onto the quarterdeck and looked out toward the southern end of the island. What he saw was a whaleboat with about a dozen men aboard, rounding the headland and pulling at their oars for all they were worth, back toward the fleet.

"They must have seen something," said Bowen.

"Beat to quarters," said Kinkaid, but there were already a lot of men with serious and resolute expressions on the deck and they quickly took their stations while others manned the guns.

As they waited in readiness another whaleboat could be seen filling with men alongside the *Royal Savage*, and it soon headed straight up the channel between the island and the New York shore.

"Looks like Arnold is sending out a scouting party, "Captain," said O'Toole.

"Probably to ascertain if they'll come down behind us," mentioned Bell.

Of course the great fear was that the British would come down the channel between the island and the shore from the north, or worse, send ships that way as well as attack them from the south, placing them in a crossfire.

In the meantime Arnold held a meeting with his two senior officers, General Waterbury and Colonel Edward Wigglesworth, but it ended rather quickly because Arnold was soon seen leaving the *Royal Savage* and going aboard the row galley *Congress*, their biggest and most heavily armed row galley.

Even before Arnold reached the *Congress* the crew aboard the *Royal Savage* could be seen raising their anchor and manning her yards and braces and she soon had her sails raised and was heading out of the bay and into the lake. Meanwhile the boat.

"Where the hell does she think she's going?" asked Bowen in consternation.

"Look, here comes a boat from the Congress," shouted Parker.

It was the same boat that had delivered Arnold to the Royal Savage to the Congress, and as it drew near an army captain hailed them and asked, "Are you the captain of the *Trumbull?*"

"Aye," answered Kinkaid.

"Orders from General Arnold! The British fleet has been spotted and he has transferred his command to the *Congress*! You are to raise sail immediately! Follow her out and you are to abide by all of her instructions!"

"Of course I shall comply!"

The *Royal Savage* was already heading out into the lake as the *Congress* hauled her anchor and Kinkaid had their ship do the same. He also noticed that the galley *Washington* had also been visited by the army captain and she too was now hauling up their anchor.

"Are we four to meet the British fleet then?" asked Sergeant Bowen.

"I'm just following orders, Sergeant," said Kinkaid with some annoyance, although wondering the same thing.

They drifted free of the anchorage and soon had their sails up and were following the *Congress* out of the bay with Jack Parker at the tiller.

"Signal flags going up on the Congress, Sir," said Parker. "Green square over blue pennant."

O'Toole had the signal book on his lap and he quickly interpreted their meaning.

"All ships: line formation."

"Man the sweeps!" ordered Kinkaid.

The *Washington* had raised her sails by now and also had her sweeps out, and she followed the *Trumbull* out of the bay, and now both ships were broad reaching to catch up to Arnold aboard the *Congress* as she led them out into the lake on a coarse of due east. In the meantime, the *Royal Savage* had caught the stiff breeze over the open water and was already well out into the lake.

The wind was gusty at first as the three row galleys left the shelter of the bay but they soon got up to speed and made good time through the light chop, and when they rounded the headland of the island Kinkaid could see dozens of ships out in the open waters of the lake to the north.

"Well, there they are," said O'Toole.

"Lordy, but so many of them," said Sergeant Bowen.

Kinkaid said nothing but picked up his telescope and had a look at the line of sails that seemed to stretch across the expanse of the lake.

The British fleet seemed not to have been organized into a recognizable formation, but all ships were heading south in front of a strong and steady north wind. Their four largest vessels were in the lead in a scattered line; the big three-masted ship *Inflexible* in the center, with the two large schooners, the *Maria* and the *Carleton* on each side of her, all heavily armed with large bore cannons. And there to starboard of the *Carleton* was that massive gunboat, the *Thunderer*. Scattered behind those were over twenty gondolas and smaller gunboats and behind those were another fleet of bateaux bringing up the rear, over thirty vessels in all. Even as he watched he saw them adjust their course so that all their bows were now pointing directly toward them.

It was an awesome sight to behold, and it seemed incredulous to Kinkaid that Arnold had sent out his best four ships to meet them, for they were badly outnumbered and outgunned. Not only that, but the British fleet enjoyed the advantage of the weather gauge, and would be free to maneuver and alter course at will.

"Now I know how the fox feels with a pack of hounds after him," said Goodman, surprising everyone by coming out of the cabin. His arm was in a sling, but he had not been able to remain below with all the excitement, and nobody could blame him for that.

Metcalf stood on the deck amidships with his mouth hanging open as if mesmerized by the sight.

Even the normally cool and brave talking Jack Parker lost his composure for a second when he asked, "What are we supposed to do against all of them, Captain?" expressing what they were all thinking.

"Mind your tiller, Parker!" shouted Kinkaid. "Another point to larboard! That's it!"

The *Royal Savage* was close-hauled and way out into the lake and was clawing her way upwind in her attempt to close with the British fleet, but the *Congress*, *Trumbull* and *Washington* were beginning to catch up to her as they formed a straight line each behind the other.

"New signals going up, Captain!" yelled O'Toole.

Kinkaid saw the two flags going up the masthead of the *Congress*.

"Green square over red triangle."

The British fleet was closing fast and would soon be within long gun range of them, and so there was a moment of tension while O'Toole flipped through the signal book once again.

Finally he looked up and said, "All ships; return!"

Sergeant Bowen audibly sighed in relief.

"Prepare to come about!" ordered Kinkaid. "Starboard sweeps cease! Hard right rudder! Bell, man those braces!"

"Now what was the point of that?" asked Bowen aloud as the men on deck scrambled to release the braces.

"Arnold just wanted to make sure they knew we were here," guessed O'Toole, and it seemed as good an explanation as any.

Their starboard oars ceased and lifted clear of the water even as Parker put the tiller over and Bell kept adjusting their sails as the ship wore about.

The weatherly *Congress* and *Washington* had deftly managed the same maneuver, but the schooner *Royal Savage*, being square-rigged, was not as maneuverable and she took some time to make her turn.

"Commence starboard sweeps!" ordered Kinkaid as they completed their turn and steadied on a course back to the shelter of the bay.

But the *Royal Savage* was still some distance behind them.

They had not only been much faster than the schooner in making their turn with their lateen sails and their sweeps out, but they were also much faster as they rode the wind back to the shelter of the bay, and as the three row galleys cleared the shallows off the southern end of Valcour Island they could see that the *Royal Savage* had been blown down the lake when she made her turn and now the strong northerly wind was against her as she tried to tack back into the shelter of the bay.

"She's missed stays," observed Parker at the tiller.

"She's in irons, all right," observed O'Toole, meaning she had not been able to buck the wind as she began her tack. In fact, her sails were blowing her backwards, farther down the lake. She would have to fall off and allow her sails to get a new grip on the wind before she could try to come up again.

In the meantime the largest of the British ships, as well as a dozen gunboats, were quickly bearing down on her, and even as Kinkaid watched he saw a row of fire and smoke issue from the side of the big three-masted ship *Inflexible* as she discharged her heavy broadside of 18-pounders at the struggling *Royal Savage*, and even at her distance he could see holes ripped through her canvas and pieces of wood fly up as the balls hit home and spouts of water erupted all around her. It was only a second or two later that the booms of the guns reached his ears.

The line of British gunboats soon drew near to her and now they began adding their loud booms to the cacophony and it was apparent that the *Royal Savage* was taking a serious pounding as she tried to slowly claw her way back toward the bay with little success.

"Dear Lord, she's missed stays again," said Parker.

"What the hell does Captain Hawley think he's doing?" growled Goodman in frustration.

"He'd be better off skedaddling down the lake," observed O'Toole.

"Pay attention there," Kinkaid reminded his crew as they neared the open space they had just left between the *New Jersey* and the *Philadelphia* where they would anchor again.

They continued to listen to the attack on the *Royal Savage* while Corporal Bell directed his sail handlers as they maneuvered into the bay, and as soon as they were securely anchored they all turned their attention back to her and all could see that she was badly damaged as she continued to work her way slowly up the lake with the gunboats of the enemy practically alongside her, their cannons booming.

Her sails were shot full of holes and her bulwarks had large gaps in them and they could only imagine the blood and horror on her decks. At least the *Inflexible* had passed her by and could not get at her at the moment, for she was downwind of her now and was having the same trouble getting back up the lake.

Even so, those gunboats with their heavy cannons and expert British and German gunners were inflicting terrible damage to the American schooner as they closed ever nearer to her using their sweeps.

"Look, she's lost a tops'l," said Bell, and they could all see that it was flapping free in the breeze, along with parted rigging and shrouds blowing out, connected to nothing.

"Well, Hawley better make his turn soon," observed O'Toole, and they all knew that any ship with a deep keel like the *Royal Savage* had to steer well clear of the shallows off the southern tip of Valcour Island, and no sooner had the words left O'Toole's mouth when they all saw the proud ship stagger and her masts bend forward.

"She's aground!" shouted Bell.

"Damn, and I thought Hawley was a great sailor," said

Goodman.

"Maybe he meant to run her aground," said Parker.

"You know, you might be right," gave O'Toole.

"Look, they're jumpin'," shouted Metcalf.

Sure enough, dozens of men could be seen leaping over the side of the stricken schooner, into the shallow water and they all started wading toward the rocks at the end of the island even as those British gunboats continued to blast her with 12 and 24-pound solid shot.

But now those British gunboats were coming within range of the line of American vessels stretched out across the bay and they all began to open up on them with a vengeance.

"Come on," yelled Kinkaid, "let's give 'em hell!"

Goodman followed Timmerman to where the 18-pounder sat and was soon encouraging the crew as they pointed her muzzle toward the neat line of gunboats.

The massive cannon had already been loaded and so all they had to do was line her up and touch her off, and when Timmerman applied the linstock they all watched as the ball landed smack dab in the center of those gunboats, sending planks and men flying everywhere, and it brought a loud cheer from the men.

"Reload!" yelled Goodman, and the men scrambled to sponge out the big gun, shove a fresh charge of powder down the barrel, ram in a new ball and then pull on the side tackles to draw her forward.

"Fire!"

Again came the violent discharge that made the entire ship shudder, and again they hit one of one of the gunboats, the ball blowing right through, killing or wounded more men.

It was now the turn of the British gunboats to take a terrible beating from the American ships that had all began to concentrate their fire upon them, and so it wasn't long before whoever was in charge of those gunboats had them spread out and reform in a line abreast parallel to the American line.

Now Kinkaid's 9 and 12-pounders along her starboard side got in on the action as the British gunboats maneuvered to their new station and soon a savage and ferocious cannon duel commenced between the two lines of opposing ships.

It wasn't long before cannon balls began whistling over the heads of the men aboard the *Trumbull,* and then the enemy boats found the range and heavy balls began to slam into their sides and the *Trumbull* began to shudder, both with the discharge of her own cannons and the pounding she was taking from the enemy guns.

Sergeant Bowen had his men working the swivel guns and they began to sweep the decks of the British boats to good effect, to the point where the line of them quickly backed off to a range of about seven hundred yards and out of the range of the swivels.

By now the smoke between the two opposing forces was thick enough to block their view of one another and so Kinkaid went from one gun to another, exhorting his crews to, "Aim careful and true and make your shots count."

Parker went down beside one of the 12 pounders in the cabin with a bad splinter wound to his right arm, and so Kinkaid took charge of aiming and firing the gun himself even as Bowen, Goodman and O'Toole took charge of the six and nine pounders amidships, the 18-pounder at the bow unable to bear on the enemy line.

It was around this time that bullets began whacking into their hull and zinging over the heads of the men on deck, and when a ball zipped by Sergeant Bowen's head he turned in consternation and asked, "Where the hell is that coming from?"

"The shore!" yelled Bell.

Sure enough, the banks were swarming with Indians, some of them right on the bank, and others were up in the trees along the bank; hordes of them in their war paint, whooping and hollering like demons. Farther up the shore could be seen the hundreds of war canoes that had brought them.

They were also on the island and while some of those men who had escaped from the grounded *Royal Savage* met a terrible fate at the hands of the Indians there, most of her stranded crew managed to swim out to some of the ships in the bay as the battle raged.

While Sergeant Bowen had his marines fire upon the Indians along the shoreline it was hot and furious down below on the gun deck as the crews there toiled at their cannons like frantic automatons in a hell of fire and smoke and noise, while the enemy balls kept slamming into their sides and some of the gun ports began to look torn and ragged from the damage sustained.

Three of their dead lay like logs on the port side gun deck, while many more had sustained splinter wounds, although most stubbornly remained with their gun after O'Toole hastily applied a bandage to staunch the bleeding, Able Seaman Parker being one of those and he quickly returned to his 12 pounders in the cabin with his right arm in a sling.

One thing that Kinkaid noticed when he looked beyond the line of British gunboats was that the British fleet's principal ships, the *Inflexible*, the schooners *Maria* and *Carleton*, as well as the monstrous gunboat *Thunderer*, after passing the island had all drifted down the lake, and they were having a hard time bucking the wind to come up, meaning that they had largely been kept out the fight. It was at least something in their favor.

But the cannon duel that was taking place between the

British gunboats with their massive guns and the American fleet in the bay raged on for hours, and after a while the bay began to look like a floating junkyard as the ships kept taking damage, with broken spars and planks and barrels and cordage all over the place, and here and there floated a body, since the practice was to toss the dead over the side to get them out of the way.

Sergeant Bowen noticed that a few cannonballs were beginning to thud into their bow and he quickly determined that the balls were coming from the *Royal Savage*.

One of the British gundalos, the *Loyal Convert*, had come up to her using sweeps and they had boarded her and were now making use of her cannons to fire upon the American fleet, and so he told Goodman about it, and then he and Timmerman once again had their 18-pounder manned and they began to fire the gun into the hull of the *Royal Savage*. The guns from the *Congress* and the *Lee* did the same and she was soon overwhelmed by cannon fire as well as grapeshot and canister that swept her deck with a deadly hail.

Well, the fire was too hot for the British aboard her and with half of them killed or wounded they too abandoned her, now a floating wreck, and those that were left somehow managed to get back aboard their own ship.

In the meantime the *Washington*, being the closest row galley to the shore, began to fire into the masses of Indians along the shore with grape and canister, and that soon had the effect of lessening the musket fire from that quarter, for most of them disappeared into the forest to escape the deadly hail of lead thrown their way.

Kinkaid was choking and practically blinded on the smoke as he helped Parker work the 12-pounders in the cabin, and his nerves and body felt benumbed by the great concussions made by their own guns as well as the enemy balls that kept slamming into the *Trumbull* as the fight raged on. Worse, he had little idea as to the condition of their own fleet by then, and so he decided to come up on deck to ascertain the situation.

He was reassured to see all of their ships and boats as hotly engaged as the *Trumbull*, but he was not encouraged to see that the *Inflexible* had managed to come upwind, and even as he watched she delivered at least two broadsides in their direction before she once again fell off and drifted downwind.

At the center of the line and only three ships over was the *Congress*, the row galley that Arnold was aboard. Since she was their largest vessel she seemed to have attracted much of the fire from the British gunboats and Kinkaid watched as balls slammed into her sides, some passing through her bulwarks, leaving jagged holes and smashing out chunks and sections of wood paneling. Her mainmast had also been shattered and the yard was dangling precariously by a single rope. Even so her guns continued to roar and deal damage to the enemy.

Next to her was the *Philadelphia*. She was quite low in the water; in fact she looked to be sinking at her anchor, although her guns too were still being worked to good effect.

When Kinkaid looked to where the *New York* was anchored he saw one of her cannons burst as it was being fired, and it was a sickening sight to see half a dozen men and pieces of men go flying.

The *Washington*, too, looked a terrible mess, holed in a dozen places and with her rigging torn asunder.

Kinkaid looked up and saw that their own mainmast had been shattered by round shot and that the yard was down on the deck, along with the furled sail attached to it where

Corporal Bell had his men place it. Next to the fallen yard and sail were five bodies, lying side by side. One of them lay on his back, his eyes open and staring at the darkening sky and as Kinkaid passed it by he realized that it was the man who had taken Solomon Dyer's place on the 18-pounder, Joshua Timmerman, their voice of wisdom.

There was Bell, aft, seeing to the shoring up of a wide hole at their stern, right at the waterline. Private Riley was there, too, hanging over the side, helping to hold a plank over the hole while Private McDuff pounded the nails home.

"How goes it Corporal?"

"Besides this big hole we've twenty or thirty others! I'm doing my best to keep track of them and shoring up what we can and keeping the pumps working, but I don't know how much more of this we can take!"

"Good work, Bell! Oh, and as much as I regret it, we'll have to remove those men amidships, if you would, Corporal."

Bell knew Kinkaid was referring to the dead. He also realized they would have no time for funerals and that they would have to be heaved over the side; and with as little fanfare as possible.

"I'll take care of it, Sir."

When Kinkaid returned to the cabin he found O'Toole there, tending to the wounded where over a dozen men lay on the deck or sat with their backs to the after bulkhead, dazed or in agony. One was lying on Kinkaid's bunk. It was Metcalf, with a bandage around his head and over one eye, and he was moaning loudly.

Parker, having taken a bad splinter wound to his right arm, and after gamely returning to help work the 12-pounders in the cabin, now shouted to Kinkaid as he passed, "We're getting low on solid shot, Sir!"

203

"Well, try to make each one count," was all Kinkaid could say.

The battle had raged for hours, for now it began to grow dark and soon the 12-pounders had ceased to fire for they did indeed run out of solid shot and the British gunboats were too far away for grape to be of much use. But the two nine pounders and three sixes on the starboard side continued to do good service and kept throwing balls at the line of enemy gunboats that were also by now quite shivered and broken, their crews severely diminished. Their fire had fallen off considerably as their men were decimated by grapeshot and their cannons knocked asunder by the solid shot of the American galleys, and it was encouraging to see that more than a few of them had drawn away and were out of the action.

But then the British schooner *Carleton* was able to tack up into the mouth of the bay and she soon anchored there, very close to the American line, which had the effect of drawing the fire of the entire American fleet, and every ship started to pound her with great fury in spite of their diminishing ammunition and almost every one of their balls were striking home.

"Brave but foolish," observed Bell as the *Carleton* began to fire her 12-pounders at the line of American ships while dozens of cannonballs caved in her sides and tore through her rigging, and she soon began to lean to starboard as her hull filled with water, and then somebody had the presence of mind to slip her anchor cable and she went drifting downwind, but by then half her crew had been killed or wounded. And then, even as she began to slide backwards, unable to steer, someone could be seen climbing out along her bowsprit, and the man began yanking on the jib so that she might have some steerageway.

But it was no use and soon two boats from the *Inflexible* were sent out to take her in tow even as she continued to take more damage from the American line.

As soon as the *Carleton* drew out of range the American ships once again directed their fire upon what was left of the steadfast line of British gunboats and it wasn't long before a powder magazine exploded aboard one of them, sending a shockwave across the bay as ammunition chests and men and pieces of wood and spars and rigging went flying high into the air.

As the debris settled the gunboat continued to burn furiously and men could be seen jumping overboard as two other gunboats drew alongside to rescue wounded survivors.

Now there burst a great fire aboard the shattered and grounded *Royal Savage* and she burned fiercely for half an hour before her own magazine exploded, lighting up the entire anchorage for a split-second in dazzling brilliance.

It was five in the evening now and growing ever darker as the gunboats began to draw away and leave the fight, but so tired and exhausted, so dazed and numb were the men by now aboard the *Trumbull* that there was not even the hint of a cheer or even any expression of relief as the battle began to wind down. Soon all of the British ships drew off and anchored somewhere down the lake while the *Royal Savage* continued to burn and the men collapsed beside their guns while O'Donnell the drummer boy went around passing out canteens to the thirsty men.

"How many have we lost?" Kinkaid asked Bowen.

"Eight killed, Captain; eleven wounded."

Kinkaid noticed that the *Philadelphia* had settled to the bottom of the bay with only her bowsprit and a bit of her stern showing above the surface, and Captain Rue and the last of her crew were being taken aboard the badly mauled

Washington.

The battle had raged for all of six hours and incredibly the *Royal Savage* and the *Philadelphia* were the only American vessels to be lost. Furthermore, in spite of the British having twice as many ships and twice the firepower not one American vessel had struck their colors.

Arnold called for all his captains to send him damage reports that night and he soon ascertained that they had lost about sixty men out of a total of 760.

He also called for another council of war with General Waterbury and Colonel Wigglesworth, and while they were satisfied that their strategy of remaining in the bay had worked to their advantage thus far, their situation remained bleak, and their prospects grim.

Almost all of the vessels were severely battered, some of them barely seaworthy. They were also critically low on ammunition, and with the likelihood that they were in for another extended battle on the morrow, and most likely against the largest British vessels, they determined that the fleet could not withstand another cannon duel with the superior guns of the British, and so Arnold ordered that the fleet was to raise anchor and slip through the British lines as best they could.

With that in mind, Arnold sent a message to the fleet, saying that it was every ship for itself and that he expected each and every captain to do all in his power to save their respective ships, to reach Crown Point with as many of them intact as possible so as to be able to continue to oppose the British advance.

Kinkaid's *Trumbull* was to lead the way.

XV

The Run South

As the *Royal Savage* continued to burn down to her waterline with all of Arnold's papers and personal effects aboard, Kinkaid found little time to contemplate the fury of the battle or consider those who had fallen, for now he had to go about the ship, rousing his exhausted and shell-shocked crew to further endeavor.

"Sergeant Bowen, can you and your men rig something so that we can raise our mainsail?"

"I can splice it with a spar, Sir."

"Do it then, and make it quick."

"Aye, Captain.

"O'Toole, we need a lantern on the stern. Be sure it's shielded on three sides so it's only visible from directly astern."

"Right away, Captain."

"Corporal Bell, how bad is the damage to our hull?"

"We're still seaworthy, Captain. Most of the holes along our waterline have been shored up and plugged and the pumps are keeping up."

"Good work, Bell."

Sergeant Bowen and his men jury-rigged their mainmast by hoisting a long spar with a block and tackle attached to the end and then wrapping it tightly with rope to the stump of the shattered mast. After securing it with sufficient standing rigging they were soon hoisting the main yard up, and Kinkaid was surprised to see Metcalf there with the bandage around his head, helping the men haul on the halyard.

"How goes it, Metcalf?"

"This damned yard hit me on the head, Captain, but I guess I'll be fine once this headache goes away."

"That's the spirit, Metcalf," said Kinkaid, patting him on the shoulder.

"Good thing there's nothing inside that iron skull of yours but empty space," joked Sergeant Bowen.

"O'Toole, since we've so little wind we'll employ our sweeps, so we'd better muffle our tholepins with rags or bits of canvas, whatever you can find."

"I'll make sure of it, Captain."

"And Parker, see that the guns are manned and ready."

"Aye, aye, Sir."

Now Kinkaid spoke to the crew on deck.

"We need to be as quiet as possible. No talking and no noise of any kind. And keep a sharp lookout."

"Are we going to give them the slip, Captain?" asked Sergeant Bowen.

"That's the idea. Now, let's haul up the anchors. Prepare to get under weigh."

It was about eight-thirty in the evening when the ship began to drift with the light evening breeze through the wreckage and bodies floating about the bay. It was a dark night with no moon, and as luck would have it they were even helped by a low-lying fog that settled over the water as Kinkaid took the *Trumbull* directly south.

It was soon discovered that their mainsail was ripped right through the middle and so it caught very little wind, but the sweeps were dipping silently into the water, moving the ship at a good rate in spite of the fading wind, as Kinkaid kept the ship about two hundred yards parallel to the western shore.

When Kinkaid looked behind him he was reassured to see a ghostly line of gundalos following in their wake, with each vessel carrying a lantern astern to help guide the next ship in line.

But Kinkaid's real concern was in front of him. Where was the British fleet? Surely they had taken the precaution of blocking their escape, and so it was with some anxiety that he peered into the gloom before them, expecting at any moment to meet with a line of gunboats that would blast them with their heavy guns at point blank range.

With only the sound of the low waves slapping against the hull Kinkaid kept the *Trumbull* on her heading of due south. It wasn't until almost an hour after they'd left the bay before Kinkaid began to think there was nothing but open water in front of them.

"Do you think we're past them, Sir?" asked Bowen.

"I believe we must be. Let's quicken our strokes now. Make all speed."

"Aye, aye, Captain."

The men began to pull at the sweeps with increased vigor now and the ship surged forward, taking advantage of the night to put as much distance as possible between them and the British fleet before first light when the enemy would catch on to the trick.

They made good time down the lake in spite of the wind

dying almost completely, and it was a little after midnight when O'Toole said, "I believe the wind is shifting, Captain."

"Yes, I was afraid of that. Loose sails; we'll proceed with sweeps only."

Already the men had been toiling at the oars for over three hours, and now their torture would be made worse by having to buck a wind that began to gust up from the south, and their progress was noticeably slowed and at times it seemed they barely made headway as the waves began to rise.

Kinkaid had them raise the sails again in an attempt to tack across the lake, and they kept having to raise and then lower the sails as the wind continued to shift erratically. And then the rope binding on the jury-rigged mainmast began to come apart, with the yard about to fall again because half the standing rigging had parted and now they had no choice but to proceed under sweeps only, giving the men no respite from their ceaseless backbreaking torture.

Kinkaid was especially impressed by Private Riley whose energies never seemed to flag, and it seemed like he had been everywhere during the battle, always lending a hand wherever he could be most useful.

"Sergeant, let's spell the men at the sweeps every hour."

"Very good, Sir."

The already exhausted men were by now almost beyond the limit of their endurance, yet still they pulled at the oars hour after hour, and by first light they could see the scattered line of their battered fleet strung out behind them, with the row galley, *Congress* and *Washington* bringing up the rear. At least a fog still hung over the lake, cutting down visibility and shielding them from the view of the British.

Arnold, aboard the *Congress*, had been the last to leave the bay of Valcour Island, but the *Washington*, with her rigging and sails badly shot up, had the worst time of it trying to make headway against the southerly wind, and so she was falling far behind. To make matters worse, both her sails ripped out later that morning, rendering them useless, and she had taken on so much water that she was barely making headway against the waves slamming into her bow, even with all her sweeps out. But worst of all was that the fog was blowing away and now they could see the British ships strung out in a line across the lake, which meant the British ships could see them. At least the enemy had failed to block their avenue of escape along the western shoreline and they were far up the lake.

At one point Corporal Bell came up to Kinkaid on the quarterdeck and said, "These waves are loosening our shoring and we're springing leaks faster than I can keep up with them, which means we're taking on more water, Sir, and the pumps are barely keeping up."

"Very well, Corporal."

The *Trumbull* had just passed Schuyler's Island, about nine miles from the site of the battle, and since his ship was far ahead of even the nearest gundalos, Kinkaid decided to pull into a small bay behind Ligonier Point and wait for the remainder of the fleet to catch up.

Even then, it was no time to rest, even as weary as they all were, but to make repairs to their mast, sails and hull, for everyone aboard knew that the British fleet would soon be after them.

"Corporal Bell, see what you can do about better staunching our leaks."

"Aye, Captain."

"Sergeant Bowen, let's get a proper mainmast raised if you can."

"I'll see to it, Sir."

"And O'Toole, let's get some men stitching that mainsail

back together."

"Aye, aye, Captain."

"I'll fix us up a big pot of soup, Captain," said Watkins, their cook.

Soon other vessels began to join the *Trumbull* at her anchorage, first the gundalos, some of which were falling apart at the seams, but it was learned that the *Spitfire* had sunk. The *New Jersey* was very badly holed and was taking on more water than she could pump out and she too came to rest in the shallows of the bay and had to be abandoned. Then two of the battered row galleys with their smashed bulwarks and gaping holes came limping in, first the *Congress* and then the *Washington* being the last and she low in the water and barely afloat. The *Lee* was missing and was presumed to be captured or sunk.

In spite of how exhausted all their crews were, after fighting a six-hour battle and then rowing all night with very little sleep for anyone for over thirty hours, all of the ships at the anchorage made good use of the time to further stem their leaks and make repairs to their masts, sails and rigging.

Arnold wrote a message to General Gates at Ticonderoga, asking him to send cannonballs and powder up to Crown Point as quickly as possible so that they might continue the fight, and also to send out a dozen bateaux to help tow the fleet against the southerly wind.

But they could all see that the British fleet was coming down the lake after them and so they could not remain where they were for very long, therefore it was just before sunset when Arnold sent the sloops *Enterprise,* with all their wounded aboard, and the sloop *Revenge*, carrying his message to Gates, down the lake ahead of the rest of the fleet.

The other vessels got under weigh late that evening, and it

wasn't until one-thirty in the morning after the last two gundalos, the *Boston* and the *Providence*, had passed that the repairs to the mainmast on the *Trumbull* was complete and Kinkaid had them weigh anchor, making her the last ship in the line now of retreating vessels.

At least the British fleet, still ten miles behind them, had to contend against the same headwinds that plagued the Americans and by early the next morning the chop out on the lake was considerable, making it nigh impossible for either fleet to beat up the lake on their close-hauled tacks.

The only course Kinkaid could take the *Trumbull* was to tack her across the lake toward the eastern shore with her sheets pulled tight and her bows slamming into the heavy waves that send freezing cold water up over her bow and flooding down the deck amidships, causing the entire ship to shake and shudder with every blow, and not a man was dry.

Rarely had men endured such hardship and suffering as they toiled at the sweeps for hour after hour, their backs aching, their hands raw and blistered, their bodies wet and cold, their stomachs growling, and their spirits flagging, wishing only to sleep and be somewhere else in their dreams.

"Lordy, I never thought I'd say this, but I wish I was in the army again," said Private Riley, straining at his oar and shivering like a leaf.

"I'm with you, Riley," said McDuff, straining next to him, his back about to give out. "Remember all that standing around we used to do?"

"Ah, it was an easy life, even when we was marchin'."

"All we had to do was carry our musket and look pretty."

"Oh, what I wouldn't give for a good march right now."

"The shame of it all was that we had it easy and didn't know it."

"Come on, boys, you can do it," said Corporal Bell, "Only a little while longer 'til your spelled and Watkins will have some more of that hot soup for you."

"I'd be happy just to dry out next his hot stove," said Riley.

"And maybe take a nap."

"Look at Metcalf over there. He's sleepin' and rowin' at the same time."

"And snorin', too. I think I'll try that, so shut up if you can, will ya Riley?"

"Right. I'll wake you when we get there."

"And then I'll sleep for a week."

At least the wind moderated somewhat during the early hours of the next morning, but if it weren't for the herculean efforts of the men pulling at their long oars all through that night they would not have made much progress.

As it was, the *Trumbull*, with her leaks under control and with her repaired mainmast and restored rigging, was able to pass the still struggling row galley *Washington* and then the *Congress*, with most of the gundalos making good progress close to the western shore, the entire fleet being scattered over a seven mile distance.

Thus far it looked like the surviving ships would make it to the relative safety of Crown Point, still twenty-five miles away, but then the fickle winds changed again and began to blow once more from the northeast, and as fate would have it that northerly wind reached the British fleet first, providing them a tailwind while the Americans still had to contend against the contrary southerly breezes, and the combination of factors enabled the British to close the distance between the two fleets very quickly indeed.

The *Washington*, being the last ship, still struggled to catch up but by late that morning the *Inflexible* and the schooners

Maria and *Carleton* were only a few miles behind her.

At least by then she began to come under the influence of the northerly winds, and Kinkaid could see that her captain, Colonel Waterbury, meant to take advantage of the wind shift by raising two additional square sails above her lateens to help drive her out of harm's way.

But even that did little good, for soon the dull booms of British cannons could be heard resounding down the lake as the enemy ships began to take her under fire at long range.

The men aboard the *Trumbull* could only watch helplessly as the British cannon shot fell all around her.

"Why doesn't Waterbury fire back?" exclaimed Sergeant Bowen in frustration.

"She can't," said O'Toole.

"She can't turn to port because she's too close to the shore," observed Bell astutely, "and if she turns to starboard they'll be on her like a pack of dogs."

The British vessels soon gained on her nonetheless and their shots began striking home. It was around nine o'clock when Waterbury decided they'd had enough.

"Look, she's striking her colors!" shouted Parker at the tiller.

It seemed somehow shameful, yet no one could blame Waterbury. His ship had been shattered and was barely afloat. With many of her crew killed or wounded, and even unable to sustain the fire of her own guns without danger of falling apart at the seams, there was no way she could have long endured the overwhelming firepower of the enemy's weight of cannon. Regardless, the *Washington* was now in British hands, her captain and crew made prisoners of war.

And now, with the already severely damaged *Congress* only a mile ahead of her the British fleet made all sail to catch her next, and it was only an hour later that the schooner *Maria*, the fastest and least damaged of the British ships, caught up to Arnold's flagship and began pounding her with broadsides of grape and solid shot, followed by the *Inflexible* which also let her have it with her heavy cannons.

Then the *Carleton* came up and it was heartbreaking to see her surrounded by the three British ships, especially since Kinkaid was too far away to render any assistance and all they could do was watch as she fought a desperate last stand fight, her eight guns and half a dozen swivels pitted against forty-four heavy bored British cannons.

Even so, Arnold fought his crippled vessel in a running battle down through The Narrows and beyond for over two hours in the most heroic fight Kinkaid would ever witness in his long career as a naval officer, constantly firing her cannons to good effect while close under the British guns, and even as four more vessels of the British fleet came up to join the fray.

"It seems impossible that she and those men can take such punishment," said Bell in awe as they watched the British balls slam into her already shattered bulwarks and the grapeshot sweep her decks and rigging, her sails in tatters.

Yet Arnold continued to tack his ship back and forth, bringing his own broadsides to bear against the enemy vessels, and now they were chasing him across the mouth of Buttonmould Bay where the once proud and determined American fleet had saluted the *Lee* and the *New Jersey* when they had come up to join them a month earlier.

By now the gundalos *Boston*, *Providence*, *New Haven* and *Connecticut* were being passed by the *Congress* and caught up in the running duel along the shoreline, and so they had little choice but to man their guns and join in the battle in spite of their own severe damage, and in spite of Arnold's specific orders that it was each ship for itself and that all captains were to do everything in their power to get their vessels to Crown Point. But now they too were fighting for their very lives and adding the dull booms of their own guns to that of the contest between the *Congress* and the big British ships.

Kinkaid's instincts were to come to their aid and so he gave the order, "Prepare to come about!"

Yet, even as the hands raced to man the halyards and braces, Kinkaid knew they had little chance of reaching the *Congress* and the others before it was too late. They were all of two miles away, on the other side of the lake, and with headwinds to contend with they would have to make a series of time-consuming tacks before they could come to their assistance. Regardless, Kinkaid felt compelled to try.

"She's turning into the bay!" observed O'Toole.

"And they're all following her!" added Bell.

All they could do was watch helplessly as the ships retreated into the bay as their masts and sails came toppling down and they began to fill with water under the horrific onslaught of almost a dozen British vessels that mercilessly fired into them at point-blank range.

Kinkaid could see that it was too late to help them as he watched the American ships run themselves aground and then saw men spilling over their sides, many of them carrying small arms that they held over their heads in the waist-deep water under a deluge of withering grapeshot and some men toppled over in the water, never to rise again.

"Prepare to wear ship!" shouted Kinkaid in frustration.

"Dear Lord, it's a slaughter," mumbled Metcalf in the waist. His bloody bandage, having come free, blew out in the breeze, revealing a nasty gash to his forehead.

As Kinkaid had the *Trumbull* turning back down the lake they all saw Arnold himself, being the last man to lower himself over the side of the gallant *Congress* and then wade through the frigid waters to the shore.

"I've never seen anything like it," said Bell.

"And you'll never see the likes of it again," observed O'Toole, and they all knew he was right.

As the *Trumbull* turned reluctantly away they could only watch as the stranded ships began to burn, having been set ablaze by their own crews to keep them out of the hands of the enemy, and it was a heart-wrenching sight to see so many vessels of their once glorious and noble fleet meet such a fate. Even so, they had left their colors flying from the shattered masts and had never struck.

The British, seemingly not satisfied with the destruction of those five vessels, remained hove to in the mouth of the bay and continued to fire their cannons with grape and round shot upon the shore where Arnold's wet and shivering crews had gathered to frantically throw up a makeshift breastworks in the event that soldiers were landed to make an assault against them.

"Cowardly bastards," said Parker.

The flames soon reached the magazine of the *Congress* and she blew up, scattering her timbers and spars all over the bay.

Only now did the British ships raise their sails again, and seeing that they would not come ashore, Arnold gathered up his crews and made for the shelter of the forest before marching with them down the lake toward Crown Point, only ten miles away.

"They're after us now!" shouted Parker.

Sure enough, having finished their business with the *Congress* and the four gundalos all of the British vessels were soon beating down the lake.

"Make all sail and man the sweeps," ordered Kinkaid.

"And I want two men at every oar!"

Soon all their oars were dipping into the water, making quick eddying circles on the surface as they raced south out of the reach of the British guns. Even so, it soon became apparent that the *Inflexible*, *Maria* and *Carleton*, with their spread of canvas, were catching up to them.

"Throw everything we don't need over the side!"

By ridding the ship of the extra weight of empty barrels, extra tools, spars, blocks and pulleys, and even the ship's stove they were able to lighten the ship enough to be able to pull ahead of the enemy ships.

They were in sight of Crown Point when it began to snow, and by one in the afternoon, as the hills and mountains on both sides of the lake turned white, they finally managed to pull under the relative shelter of the guns there. When they looked back they could see that the British ships had given up the chase and were heading back up the lake.

The sloops *Enterprise* and *Revenge* also made it there, as well as the only remaining gundalo, the *New York*, under the command of Captain Lee. The *New Jersey*, having thought to have sunk sometime during the retreat was later found in an obscure bay by the British and taken captive.

It turned out that Captain Davis of the row galley *Lee* had run his ship up the Onion River and set her afire before abandoning her, but the fire must not have taken because she was ultimately captured by the British and made a part of their fleet. But the schooner *Liberty* was still at Crown Point, and the newest of their row galley's, the *Gates*, was also there, having been completed too late to join the battle.

So many of their ships had been lost during the harrowing chase, but even so Kinkaid felt some measure of satisfaction in having saved the *Trumbull*, his very first command, from a similar fate. Even more than this he felt an inordinate pride in the men under his command who so unstintingly gave of themselves to fight and then safely bring her back to base in one piece.

It was a few days later when Arnold and his bedraggled crews came slogging out of forest, and never before was seen such a tattered and disheveled group of men who nonetheless received an ovation of cheers as they marched with honor through the gates of Fort Ticonderoga.

Aftermath

Having lost most of his ships, Arnold's proud fleet was decimated by the might of British power, although a perusal of many of the British officer's journals who participated in the lake battles gave high praise to General Arnold for his daring and courage under fire, a rare thing indeed for professional soldiers who considered the Americans common rabble.

Crown Point was set ablaze and abandoned for fear that the British would lay siege to it and they would needlessly lose too many men, and all assets were necessarily concentrated at Fort Ticonderoga where Arnold led a furious effort to improve his defenses against an overwhelming British force.

General Carleton took what remained of the fortifications at Crown Point and began to move some of his army there, yet, in spite of his victory over the American fleet, he then decided to call off his attack against Fort Ticonderoga after overestimating American strength there and having determined that a siege under winter conditions would be too costly. He also released under parole the captain of the *Washington*, General Waterbury, along with 110 captured American prisoners.

Spurious claims were later brought against Arnold, saying that he had abandoned many of his wounded crewmen aboard the burning *Congress*, first started by the British after the battle on the lake but then taken up by Americans who should have known better after Arnold defected.

Ultimately, Arnold was successful in doing what he had set out to do. By building and fighting an American fleet for control of Lake Champlain, he was able to hold the British at bay for another fighting season, giving the colonies time to better prepare for General John Burgoyne's summer offensive down the lakes which resulted in a major defeat for the British when General Arnold himself, and against orders, led the troops at Saratoga to a victory over Burgoyne's seven thousand man army. It was a victory that enabled Benjamin Franklin to convince the French to come into the war on our side, ultimately leading to the final showdown at Yorktown where a French fleet blocked British assistance and reinforcements, causing Cornwallis to surrender and bringing a close to the war.

As for Kinkaid, he returned to Philadelphia where, with a dearth of shipboard positions, he was given a cushy assignment as a liaison officer in charge of procurements and diplomatic duties before he was made the First Lieutenant aboard the new frigate *Randolph*.

Made in the USA
Lexington, KY
23 January 2018